♠ LOOKING ♦ GLASS ♣ CALL ♥
The

ONE FLIGHT ✈ FICTION ™

The
♠ LOOKING · GLASS ♣ CALL ♥

W. H. JOHNSON

© 2006 W. H. Johnson

All rights reserved. No part of this book may be reproduced in any form or by any means without permission in writing from the publisher, Banda Press International, Inc., 6050 Stetson Hills Blvd. #313, Colorado Springs, Colorado 80922. The views expressed herein are the responsibility of the author and do not necessarily represent the position of Banda Press International, Inc.

This is a work of fiction. The characters, names, incidents, places, and dialogue are products of the author's imagination, and are not to be construed as real.

Edited by David Abbott

Printed in the United States of America
First Printing: June 2006

Library of Congress Control Number: 2006925667

ISBN-13: 978-0-9773175-4-7
ISBN-10: 0-9773175-4-4

And so we started on that hidden road back to the sunlit world; and not caring for any rest, we climbed up, he leading and I following, so far that through a round opening I saw some of the beauties that Heaven holds, and thence we issued forth to once more behold the stars.

Dante, INFERNO, XXXIV

Prologue

I write this in my eighty-second year, not because it must be read, but because it must be written. Six decades as what kindly may be called an itinerant teacher, comforter and amateur magician have taught me the frailties of human focus and retention, much as my thousands of hours with the disturbed and dying have shown me the inevitable break-up of whole and coherent memories into living shards that flash within view like leaping trout, only to vanish below the surface, leaving no trace of their full scope or direction.

As I sit here in my study, our youngest grandchild is downstairs, struggling through one of my favorite old songs on the upright piano.

"Once in the dear, dead days beyond recall,
When on the earth the mists began to fall . . ."

This memoir may prove to be no more than "just a song at twilight," the twilight of my grip on things past. Yet I will write to keep these events intact and visible before me during the few remaining days of my life, since they have so directed and defined that life. Otherwise, I might have only this worn, little Ottoman coin to cling to at my end.

What I do not wish to keep, of course, is anger. Among whatever good I have been allowed to sow on this earth, I have raised in its shadow an undergrowth of that bitter weed by choosing to serve as a thorn in the backside of the privileged and pious, despite myriad lessons that rage grinds down to the poorest and loneliest of meals, along with much else to be revisited here.

And so I do not record this to be proclaimed abroad as gospel but simply to return to my own youthful awakening for the pure pleasure of reliving and holding it before me. Yet any friend or stranger who cares to read on is welcome.

Autumn, 1963

1

Most of my friends and family are aware that I began my college studies in Carlisle, Pennsylvania. What is less known, however, is that in the spring of 1902, my junior year, I became disillusioned with theology and deserted my studies. I had long thought of myself as a potential leader of a flock, but in the harsh light of that cold spring I felt naked and exposed, able to offer no more than a way with words and a desire for attention. I was a sham. It was too late to switch to the Applied Science curriculum, and the humiliation of facing my family and friends back in Ohio was terrifying. Accordingly, I packed up and took a train to Baltimore, the nearest large city.

In those years, Baltimore was a teeming railroad center and seaport. Its inner harbor was crowded with international steamships taking on lumber and cotton and by fleets of small sailing craft bringing daily mountains of fish, crabs and oysters from the Chesapeake Bay to packing houses which lined the waterfront. The cobblestone streets were jammed with wagons and horse-drawn trolleys that clopped and rumbled across swaths of train track past beautiful brick or stone churches and palatial homes garnished with black filigrees of wrought iron. Even today, over half a century and two World Wars later, people talk about rows of white marble steps fronting the attached houses and how maids and housewives would scrub them each morning, like a prayer to the powers of commerce and cleanliness.

    I took a room with two meals a day at a boarding house far enough away from the docks to avoid unsavory characters and went in search of work. This I found as an advertising salesman for the Baltimore Evening News, walking the streets and taking paid notices from small importers, haberdashers, saddlers and the like. My pay was exclusively commissions, and a rather poor tithe at that. Nonetheless, I found the freedom and bustle of my new surroundings to be invigorating and went about my rounds with an enthusiasm that brought me to the attention of my superiors. There I let it be known that I had attended college, more of a rarity in those years, and that I harbored a desire to see something of myself in print beyond retail ads. Accordingly, I was sent upstairs to see a fellow no older than I who encouraged me to submit a few of my articles. I had no articles at the time but threw myself fully into creating something of note.

Over the next few weeks I paced the floor of my room, disturbing the couple below, and produced several pieces that I thought showed originality and depth. These, my philosophical writings as I regarded them, were rejected outright. I learned quickly that a good description of a domestic row or some comic event was more likely to see print. Such I would carry upstairs past hat racks and spittoons into the editorial room where I would swim through a fog of cigar smoke to the desk of Wilson, the assistant editor. Here I would stare at the part in the middle of his hair until he would glance up, snatch whatever I held out and start over it with his pencil, changing words and crossing out whole sentences of "collegiate claptrap" as he called it. If the remainder was acceptable, he would grunt then scribble a note on a small ticket. This I would take to the business office downstairs, and a fee would be added to my weekly pay account. I recall clearly that one such payment was all of sixty-eight cents, enough in those days for a full course meal at a fine downtown hotel.

Two features of my life in that period are now lost in time, and with them, much of the youthful foolishness that swept me along. One was a pen name I devised for myself with which I signed all my trivial articles – Otis Elkerlick. Otis I derived from the

Greek "Outis", meaning "no man", the name Ulysses called himself in order to trick the Cyclops. Elkerlick I derived from a Dutch original on which the English morality play Everyman was based. Thus, I was no-man-every-man, and while my trivial pieces were printed under no name at all, still I thought myself quite learned and clever.

The other lost feature was Baltimore itself as I knew it, for a hellish fire destroyed most of the town in 1904, especially the side streets of small establishments where I paid my sales calls, leaving only a few structures here and there among acres of smoking ash, much as singular events continue to stand clear and whole in the drifting haze of an old person's memory.

One such structure I well remember was a carpentry workshop (I believe it was a carpentry workshop) with a narrow set of stairs at one side to a separate establishment above. This upper room was a magic shop, a magician's emporium offering all sorts of clever devices to fool the eye and amaze one's friends, a marked contrast with the acrid skepticism of that other upper room where Wilson held sway. Here, behind half-drawn blinds, one could buy a variety of hats and boxes with false linings, scarves that changed color when turned inside out, pictures that appeared and disappeared when held in a certain light, decks of secretly marked cards and a number of instruction books full of parlor tricks.

On my first visit I was mesmerized for over an hour in this dark, little shop. I finally left with one of the books and a small apparatus resembling an egg cup that turned a white marble into a black one and vice versa.

In the weeks following I would return here many times and build a small collection of the less expensive items. Alone in my room, I performed before imaginary audiences of astonished onlookers, much as I had once envisioned myself swaying rapt congregations. Soon, I was amazing my fellow boarders after dinner and distracting the young shop girls along my rounds. I avoided all tricks with playing cards owing to their tinge of gambling, yet I smile now to recall how devilish I thought myself.

It seems to me that about this same time, stage magicians, or illusionists as they were careful to call themselves, were becoming a national fascination. I remember the names of Carter, Thurston, von Aux, Roscoff and the like, not to mention the great Harry Houdini. They or ones like them came to the many theatres and lecture halls of Baltimore, and whenever I could afford it, I would study their every move from a back row seat as they floated women in mid-air or evaporated them behind drawn curtains or slipped out of shackles and handcuffs with ease. After, I would return to my room, determined to improve my innocent repertoire.

And so it was just at this time that I stumbled over something and fell into a series of events that would change my life forever, turning me inside out like a trick handkerchief and making the earth, as I had been treading it all my young life, seem false as the floor of any magician's trunk.

It was my habit then to drop by the Evening News editorial office, sit on a wooden bench by the door and peruse recent issues of newspapers that came by express mail train from larger cities like New York, Philadelphia and Boston. Often, there were ads or reviews of illusionists who had come through Baltimore in the past or might be coming soon. I also studied advertising in general, looking for new ideas or clever wording that I might steal outright to improve my own poor text.

One June morning, over a copy of the old New York World, my eye fell on an article describing an upcoming conference of professional and advanced amateur magicians to be hosted by a resort hotel in upstate New York: "Leger-de-main Legion to Let Looking Glass Lake" or some such snappy headline. A number of well-known performers were to give demonstrations, teach techniques and perhaps even compete. Glancing at the top of the page I calculated that this was to begin in just two days! I leaped from the bench and started toward Wilson's desk even before my idea was fully formed.

"Look at this," I said and thrust the article at him. He took it in at a glance.

"We don't cover rural New York," he growled. "Anyway, it's just a way for some snooty hotel to fill up empty rooms."

"Yes," I said, "but this is international news about world-famous performers. And they all come to Baltimore sooner or later. The only reason they're meeting up there is probably to keep out the general public. This will make a great story!" I was almost shouting.

By now my idea was fully formed. I was only a fledgling magician, but I would get myself up there using the newspaper connection. My words seemed to hang in the tobacco smoke as Wilson puffed his cigar once, then again, a good sign with him. One puff augured dismissal of an idea; two indicated extensive, if rapid, cogitation. It had to be my excitement and a blind conviction that I was the paper's man for this task that gave me courage at that moment, for I heard myself say, "I'll need an advance for the train fare and hotel."

Wilson puffed a third time, snatched the paper from my hand and darted into the chief editor's office behind him. He was back in a minute, scribbling a voucher.

"Fifteen dollars even," he said. "Train, hotel

and meals for a day. If we can't use your piece, you'll have to owe us. Wire ahead, and show 'em this so they don't take you for a college boy on a prank." He tossed a press pass toward me, my first and only.

The article had said the convention was to last three days, and I decided on the spot that I would find some way to stay the whole time regardless. As I went toward the door, Wilson called after me.

"And no alcohol!"

It wasn't necessary to tell me that, but I smiled. A good deal of Evening News capital was spent in bars and taverns, no small amount by Wilson himself. But I was already drunk with excitement, and running downstairs I pulled my cap rakishly to one side.

I collected my advance then stopped at the telegraph office to wire the hotel and let them know I was coming as a member of the press. The form had a signature line at the bottom. I paused and glanced at the press pass Wilson had given me. The name line was still blank. I took a deep breath and signed both — Otis Elkerlick.

2

Perry could not have calculated his polar expedition more carefully than I planned my trip during the next twenty-four hours. A dollar of my own savings went for a new, felt derby in a dashing but dignified brown. I would carry only a small travel bag similar to one I had seen used on stage. My collection of magic apparatus would be left behind lest it betray me as a novice. Just a few books for quick reference in the privacy of my hotel room would be my provisions. A reporter's pad and pencil would be my armament. A few extra dollars of my own would be pinned inside the waistband of my trousers, for I had seen remarkably deft pick pocketing in one particular performance. I, however, would be prepared. Gazing into the hallway mirror, I regarded myself as the light cavalry of modern journalism.

"Elkerlick of the Baltimore Evening News," I said to my reflection and repeated it snappily to myself a score of times before finally going to bed.

It may have been the poor night's sleep or just the gossamer confidence of untried young men, but walking to the train depot in the early dawn, I felt an urge to turn back and twice nearly tripped on the cobblestones.

Aboard, I sat in a back corner of the coach, wondering if reporters would be welcomed where I was going. What if they weren't? I hadn't bothered to ask anyone. Surely the hotel would have answered my wire. Could I just walk into any meeting and sit down? What if I were restricted to eavesdropping in the hallways? Maybe I would step in front of people to ask bold, penetrating questions. Or should I remain just the one day and write some pabulum or other? Would I have the nerve to stick it out and get to the bottom of things? "Elkerlick of the Baltimore Evening News," I groaned to myself. I might as well say I'm Captain Jinx of the Horse Marines. When the train reached Jersey City, I saw that I had barely noticed the stops in Wilmington and Philadelphia and had completely forgotten the sandwiches stuffed into the side pockets of my jacket.

Northbound trains didn't stop in Manhattan then since there was no bridge or tunnel across the Hudson River. The Baltimore and Ohio ended in Jersey City, and I remember crossing an overhead walkway to catch an Albany spur of the New York

Central. I was waiting there, holding a half-eaten sandwich and thinking of my people in Ohio when a fellow just a few years older than I came up and sat at the far end of my bench.

He seemed something of a dandy. I recall the jaunty angle of his derby, his checkered vest and a pair of glossy, tan spats. His cardboard valise was covered with stickers. Without looking in my direction, he took out a pack of cards, or rather it suddenly appeared in his hand at a quick flick of his wrist. He shuffled them in mid-air, spun the pack rapidly between his two index fingers like a paddle wheel, then stretched them apart and back several times like a concertina.

I was transfixed. The cards were a single, solid piece in his hands, in one instant a stretch of cloth, in the next a fistful of fluttering taffy, folding and refolding as if stuck to his fingers. He did this automatically, gazing out over the tracks, much as one might idly brush away an insect. Suddenly he stopped, looked at the deck in his palm as if just noticing what he had been doing, then clapped his hands together. The cards vanished as they had appeared.

"Bravo," I said aloud.

He turned to me for the first time, smiled and touched his hat brim. Then scooping up his valise, he stepped behind some pillars and disappeared like his miraculous cards.

Since that day so long ago I have learned a hundred times over that signs and omens rarely tumble down from some celestial throne on high. Rather, they tend to arise from a source placed within each of us and speak only in some still, small voice. Nonetheless, at that moment I held no doubt that fate was directing my journey and that my fledgling interest in magic had aroused some dark demiurge to materialize this fellow before my eyes in order to draw me onward. When the train arrived, I hopped on, picked out a pair of empty seats facing each other, propped up my feet and once again was Elkerlick of the Baltimore Evening News.

The Albany route of that line runs alongside the Hudson River. Framed by the window at my side, an endless gallery of live paintings passed before me, some with small boats in the foreground, others fading off to distant farmhouses. The calming effect must have lulled me to sleep, because I was suddenly awakened by a tap on my shoulder. I turned my head and found myself staring at a checkered vest.

"Corinth coming up. Our stop," he said.

I must have looked dumbfounded. Where was I? Was this fellow real? And how did he know? Perhaps he read my mind because he smiled and pointed to my ticket that hung from the clip above my seat.

"You're going to the conference perhaps?" he asked.

I mumbled that I was.

"Then you are a brother of the art," he said.

That took me a second. "No," I said." I work for a newspaper." (At that moment, my bravura was still asleep.)

"Ah," he said. "A gentleman of the press." With that, and minus an invitation, he sat down on the seat facing me, laid his hat carefully beside him and leaned forward with a hand on each of his knees. I noticed that he had a thick shock of coppery red hair.

"And what newspaper may I ask?" he said.

Beside the noticeable hair, this fellow had beautiful white teeth and a manner of pausing before each sentence with his lips parted and his chin raised, as if posing in a stage light.

"Baltimore Evening News," I said. And then, as if to plunge in to get it all out, I said, "Otis Elkerlick of the Baltimore Evening News."

"Ah," he repeated. "Do you have a card, Sir?"

I thought he meant the press pass and was reaching for it but caught my mistake. He was offering me a calling card that had suddenly appeared between two of his fingers. I took it and read "Antoine Junius Maurel, Illusionist. New York, London, Paris, Rome."

"You get around," I said. "Are you French?"

He struck his pose again, paused a second as if

for effect and replied, "My homeland is the stage, but I have played several houses in Baltimore. You must know."

I didn't know, even though I had been reading the papers for some time. It didn't occur to me then that he might have been lying or that the name on his card was only a stage name.

"I couldn't help noticing your skill with the playing cards back there," I said.

"Playing cards?" he asked, patting all his pockets. "Don't seem to have mine about me. May I borrow yours?" He thrust his hand into my jacket pocket, now empty of its sandwich, and produced the deck of cards.

"Why these are mine," he exclaimed, feigning an air of shock. "Now really, Sir . . . ."

I grinned with embarrassment as the train began to slow down. Maurel rose to get his valise from across the aisle then stood back with a slight bow and waved me ahead of him. Carrying my bag to the end of the car, it began to dawn on me that I represented the power of the press, however fraudulently, and my attention might be worth something to these people.

Thirty or forty travelers, mostly men, were debarking with us. Maurel tipped his hat and spoke to several. If all these were performers, I thought, they looked ordinary enough out of evening dress. Beyond the depot, two old-fashioned station wagons stood waiting, horse-drawn busses with canvas awnings that could roll down and wooden slat sides that read "Looking Glass Lake Hotel."

The first wagon had already filled and the driver was snapping his reins when we ran for the last two seats of the second. Maurel tossed up our luggage, climbed in and offered me his hand. In the corner of my eye I saw a hatless and bearded old fellow in a rumpled suit step back as though he had meant to board, but having seen that my companion and I were together and that only two seats remained, was sacrificing his chance. I didn't bother to thank him.

As we pulled out, Maurel was expanding with what he knew about this place.

"It's a very exclusive retreat," he said, "familiar to the finest families. I've heard that ordinary guests must be recommended. Bringing our art here is something of a coup. Do you know that motorcars are not allowed? And there's an observation tower from which you can see the entire mountain range, or so I'm told. What's more, no one enters or leaves on Sundays. Fancy that," he said. "And no alcohol."

I had to laugh aloud at that echo of Wilson's parting admonition, and as I turned to glance back at the depot, I saw the old fellow in the rumpled suit lift his bag to his shoulder and begin trudging behind us up the long mountain road.

3

To this day I recall how the winding course up that mountain resembled a magician's act. The forest on each side was well into late spring leaf so that sunlight flickered over us like gas lighting. By turning every few yards, the road concealed what lay just ahead only to surprise us every minute or so, at first with sudden sprays of wild blossoms, then huge outcroppings of riven granite, and finally with ancient oaks that loomed out at us like bands of gnarled druids. I thought of Dante, lost in his medieval wood, and tried to imagine Maurel as my Virgil, leading me upward, not downward, into some inferno. He had been rattling on beside me and now broke into my reverie with a question.

"Do you know Zoromagus? His work, I mean."

I had to admit that I didn't.

"Maestro Zoromagus is the magician's magician," he said, then added in a whisper, "not your vaudeville medicine show tricksters like most of these. He works only select audiences, which is why this is such a special occasion."

"He wasn't mentioned in the news article," I said.

Maurel shrugged. "Those who know, know," he said. "He's been mostly in Europe and Russia the last few years."

"What's so special about him?" I asked.

Maurel struck his pose again for a moment then launched into a florid description of the art and technique of this Zoromagus. Of mysterious origin and trained in Egypt and the Near East, this fellow seemed to have been the friend and private wizard to any number of sultans and czars, curing diseases and predicting the future. Somewhere along the line it came to be understood by those inside some magic circle or other that he was the fountainhead of all known magical lore and that all stage illusion practiced today could be traced to him. Maurel was beginning to sound like a carnival pitchman.

"This fellow must be over a hundred years old," I said smiling.

Maurel snorted. "He's ageless if you must know. I tell you these things because I thought you came here to gather information. I'll have you know that he's been instrumental in arranging this very conference."

"You know a great deal about him," I said, trying to be amicable. "Have you met him?"

"Twice," he explained. "First in Lisbon and then at Padua a year ago. That's when he told me of this event. I promised to be here and to study under him."

"You're sort of a disciple then," I said.

"Yes," he replied. "Disciple. That's a good word."

"But what about some of the other famous ones?" I asked. "Won't they show up here too? Harry Houdini, for example."

Maurel suddenly spat over the side of the wagon. "Erich Weiss you mean? That little Yiddish poseur? His kind isn't welcome at a place like this."

We fell silent as I thought over Maurel's last remark. Outrageous as it may seem to younger people, many private resorts and hotels once practiced a far less tolerant policy than today. I suppose the intent was to heighten their perceived quality somehow by turning away certain guests, for in addition to excluding people of color and unwed couples they often rejected any woman known to have been divorced and all members of the Jewish race. Such a possibility had not occurred to me before that moment, and I puzzled over why an event like this would be held in a place that would exclude any number of skilled performers.

I was still lost in thought as the wagon made a steep descent for several minutes, then made a sharp turn between two enormous oaks and rolled to a stop in a cliff-side clearing to give us our first stunning view. It was Looking Glass Lake and its exclusive hotel.

I had seen pictures of such places, real and imagined, in books, and since then have witnessed them myself in northern Italy and the Bavarian Alps. But that afternoon, looking out at that enormous, enclosed basin of mountain walls, tumbled boulders and dark water I felt like Peer Gynt entering the Hall of the Mountain King.

The hotel stood ahead to our right and seemed to rise directly from the water's edge six or seven stories, ending in conical roofs resembling elfin caps. Delicate, skeletal balconies covered the front, stacked rib-like, one above the other. These, like the wooden siding, had taken on the granite grey of the surrounding cliffs where evergreens jutted like tusks from cracks in the rock face. At the base of the building was an enormous, covered veranda reaching out over the water on pylons, and from just below this, three long boat docks splayed further out, like a gigantic bird's foot. This seemed to press down on a reflection of the hotel, which shimmered like a vaporous banner just beneath the lake surface.

The lake itself was well named. In the afternoon glare, it resembled silvered glass. About a hundred yards wide, it stretched nearly a mile forward like the floor of a gigantic coliseum between natural stone pilasters, many with huge boulders balanced at the foot, as if frozen in some ancient avalanche. One such pile on the shore directly opposite the hotel had a precarious-looking wooden catwalk built out over it. The cliffs to either side were terraced with clumps of cedar strung together by handrails along pathways set into the rock and little, shingled gazebos perched at intervals. This network seemed to ply its way upward along the lake canyon sides toward the far end.

There a single structure cut into the sky. The first sight of it seemed to pull me straight up onto my feet. It was the famed observation tower, a gaunt, stone structure, rising many stories above the distant treetops, like some buried giant's finger raised in promise or warning.

I was spellbound, but the spell was broken when our wagon started up again, tumbling me back onto the seat. We jostled another hundred yards or so along the shoreline then came to a stop in the hotel carriageway between a formal garden and the side of the veranda. Several young men in livery appeared and began to take down our luggage, carrying it onto the veranda and through the main entrance. I carried my own bag since I didn't have any tip money to spare.

Inside, I stepped away from the file of newcomers to get my bearings.

As my eyes adjusted, I took in a broad room with dark wooden floors and polished oak trim. It was not a lavish foyer like the Baltimore hotels with high, gilt ceilings and crystal chandeliers. Rather, I recall how the shuttered afternoon sun gave a fiery glow to the dark red carpet and papered walls as though they were embers fanned by the large sets of blades turning slowly overhead at the end of a connecting shaft and belt apparatus.

At one side of the room was the hotel registration desk where a crowd was already gathering. At the other was a carved library table and next to it stood a tall, patrician-looking fellow with white hair and a pink face. He wore a cutaway coat with a red carnation like a fancy church usher and, apparently, was our host representing the hotel. Beside him was an easel with a signboard announcing the conference.

This will be the test, I thought. I walked up to him and presented my press pass. He seemed neither pleased nor annoyed but simply ran his thumb down a long roster of names on a sheet of paper then shook his head.

"Do you plan to attend the sessions?" he asked.

"Of course," I said. "Are there any other reporters here yet?"

"None," he answered. "We haven't encouraged it. You'll need to purchase a guest ticket."

I paid him two of my precious dollars. With the ribbon he gave me in my lapel, I crossed over to register for my room. Here was a problem. At first my wire hadn't been received at all, and then it had arrived too late.

"I've come all the way from Baltimore on a special assignment," I huffed, and flashed my press pass between two fingers as I had seen Maurel do with his card. The clerk stared at me as though I were a hired arsonist on an assignment. Finally, he went to the far end of the counter and returned with a key.

"There's a room available on the seventh floor," he said. "You'll have to walk the last flight."

"No matter," I snapped. "How much?"

"Five dollars a day," he said. "Dining privileges included, of course."

I froze. This seemed an atrocious sum. Worse, it was only Thursday. The convention would conclude on Sunday, and since the station wagons didn't run on that day of rest I would have to stay four nights to attend the whole event. My fifteen dollar advance and personal savings had already been depleted by the round-trip train fare and now by the guest membership. I calculated that I had enough to cover two full days but was short for a third and fourth. Nonetheless, it was too late to back down now.

"I'm expected in New York City Saturday evening," I said, and thought to myself that a lie might not count as such at a convention of illusionists. The clerk watched curiously as I signed the register.

"Elkerlick," he mused.

"Yes," I said, "Dutch," and snatched up the key.

The elevator, a cubicle chamber of polished oak, was one of the old hydraulic powered types. The operator controlled it by pulling against one or the other of two ropes that ran vertically through the floor and roof in a corner of the chamber. When we stopped at the mezzanine level, a lady and two gentlemen got on. The men were carrying their hats, and I realized, to my embarrassment, that I had not removed my precious, new derby since entering the hotel.

From the sixth floor I climbed a set of stairs up to a narrower hall where workmen had left a trestle table standing. There were scraps of wallpaper lying about and several buckets of paste. I squeezed past, went a few doors beyond the lavatory and found my room at the end.

It was small but pleasant enough, possibly intended just for servants under normal circumstances. (A few wealthy folk traveled with personal attendants in those days.) It had a small window facing out the rear of the hotel toward the cliffs and mountains beyond. I arranged my few items on the bureau top, stuck a notepad and pencil in my pocket and went downstairs to take up the serious business of journalism.

I knew no one here other than Maurel, and he had disappeared on our arrival. It was too early for dinner, so I explored the various parlors on the mezzanine level. One was a large music room, I supposed, with a square grand piano and semi-circles of plush couches. Across the hall were two smaller rooms, both libraries, one with writing desks discretely tucked in each corner and equipped with inkwells, steel pens and hotel stationery. The second contained a dozen or so wing chairs set at random angles, a rack of newspapers and a wall of books behind leaded glass doors. I noted leather-bound editions of Dickens and Emerson such as I had seen at college, also a number of illustrated Bibles and a copy of the New York Social Register.

At its end, the mezzanine hallway opened into a long, narrow room that stretched both right and left across the front of the hotel with windows looking out under the roof of the veranda toward the lake. On one side were chess and checker tables, each with a set of pieces in a lined box. Card tables filled the other side, for whist players, I guessed. (Bridge was not very well known yet.) A new, unopened box of playing cards lay on each like a hard, square cake of soap.

Finally, there was a set of stairs down to a windowless room that smelled like Wilson's cigar. Here were two billiard tables and a rack of cues. The tables were without pockets, indicating that this was no low-life pool hall, yet it seemed apparent that ladies rarely set foot here.

Back upstairs, guests were filing down the hall toward dinner, and I followed them into a large, columned room of round banquet tables. I took a seat near a back corner next to a pleasant-looking couple from out west –- Chicago, I think. The man was an amateur magician, "a dilettante in the best and original sense of the word," he explained. His wife seemed to nod at everything he said and assured me that her husband was quite talented.

"What do you know of this Zoromagus?" I asked to make conversation.

He fished up a program booklet from inside his jacket, and I realized that in my nervousness at the admission table I had failed to pick up a copy.

"He's one of the main demonstrators, I believe," he said squinting at a page held out before him. "Supposedly a hypnotic speaker too. I've seen his name in print but can't say I've ever seen or read much about him."

"Sidney reads a great deal," his wife put in. "Books, newspapers, magazines. Why, just hundreds and hundreds of pages." She nodded a few more times for emphasis. I excused myself before the dessert.

But crossing the room, I noticed Maurel at another table. He spotted me as well. And just as I reached the door, I saw him lean forward quickly to say something to his companions.

4

The fellow in the cutaway coat had left the foyer by now, but some of the program booklets lay about on the table. I took one and went up to my room to study it. This was a curious little book, and I would still have it today except for all that happened later. It was tall and thin like a railroad timetable, perhaps suitable for concealing up one's sleeve. Its title, The World of Illusion, was printed in a circle around a line sketch of an attractive young woman who appeared as a hag when viewed differently.

The contents listed the events of Friday through Sunday with simultaneous, small sessions in the mornings and general sessions in the afternoons and evenings. This resembled a young men's career exposition I had once attended except that here the speakers had inflated titles: "The Great and Mysterious Whosis" or "The Incomparable So and So." A few had Chinese or Arabic names added in parentheses. The sessions had stars and triangles beside them to indicate the degree of expertise attendees were expected to have. The back cover was printed with long vertical lines so that when one tilted the booklet flat like a table and looked at it from the edge, the word "Silence" became visible, the illusionist's creed, I assumed.

But looking over the schedule I saw my dilemma. Here it was Thursday evening. The major presenters, including Zoromagus, were scheduled for Saturday afternoon. The formal banquet was that same evening. Sunday afternoon was to be given over to competitions at various levels with a lantern party and award ceremony on the veranda that evening to conclude the whole affair. And here I could pay for only two days at the hotel and would have to leave Saturday after breakfast. I didn't care about the banquet and couldn't have attended anyway since I hadn't brought any formal evening attire (a requirement in those days). But missing the best performances and the competitions would be a disaster, not only for my own interest, but for the fascinating article I was supposed to produce.

What to do? They hadn't been especially friendly at the registration desk. I didn't dare wire Wilson for a second advance, and for a member of the press to borrow money from a near stranger would be ludicrous and humiliating. I paced the tiny area of my room and finally stomped all the way downstairs to walk off my frustration.

It was after dusk by now. Out on the veranda a few guests sat around tables with coffee or lemonade. A group of men had gathered, showing each other card tricks. I walked past them to the railing and was staring moodily down at the water when I noticed a man and woman down below on one of the boat docks. They had a young girl with them, the only child I had seen here. She was tossing pieces of dinner roll into the lake and laughing with delight each time as a dozen or more large trout would suddenly foam up in a beautiful burst of silver then disappear again under the dark water.

Why couldn't some stranger simply toss me the extra I needed, I thought. Even these fish are able to stay as guests of the hotel. "Foxes have holes, and birds of the air have nests," I waxed to myself, "but the son of man hath no where to . . . ."

At that time in my life, so many years ago, I had yet to grasp the degree to which I could be possessed wholly and instantly by an idea. Indeed, for most people such a thing is no more than a turn of phrase. But for me, it has been a deeply defining trait, as pronounced as a large birthmark or a twin sibling, and was especially so in that open and expectant period of my young manhood.

Looking down at the water that evening I

suddenly knew how I would solve my problem. The physical impact of my idea gave me a sense that some mysterious personal force flowed out of me so that the railing under my hands seemed charged with a current, and my legs had become the pylons supporting the veranda till I thought myself rising from the lake bottom like a titan.

I was going to stay for the whole conference! On Saturday, I would simply check out as scheduled then stash my bag in the woods nearby and return to the hotel wearing my admission ribbon. I would sleep two nights under the trees. The weather promised to be fair, and so long as I didn't appear in the dining room, my extended stay would go undetected. I returned to my room a different fellow, nodding and smiling at everyone I passed along the way.

Preparations for my plan went into effect at Friday's breakfast when I slipped some biscuits into my pocket. "Feeding the fish," I said to a lady who looked at me curiously.

That morning I attended a session on parlor tricks involving numbers and took copious notes from a blackboard, much like old school days. Next was a session on trick knots where we each were given a piece of rope. I had a hard time going back and forth between the notes and the knots. By the midday meal, however, my skills had improved, and I caused a large bunch of grapes to disappear inside my jacket. When

I returned to my room to add these to my little stash, I found a note on one of Maurel's cards stuck in the doorjamb.

"Your presence is cordially solicited for the demonstrations to be held in the Viennese Parlor at two today. A.J.M." it said.

I went, of course. The Viennese Parlor turned out to be the music room with the square, grand piano. Maurel was not mentioned in my program booklet, but I had no doubt that he would be giving a performance and intended for me to see it. The piano had been draped with a tasseled tablecloth. A dozen or so fresh packs of hotel playing cards lay on top.

The room was already crowded, and we latecomers were lining up along the back wall behind rows of couches when the conference host in the cutaway coat marched in, leading a column of six or seven men. Maurel stood out among them with his coppery hair. The crowd fell silent, and it was announced that we were about to witness an afternoon of amazing card tricks and mental telepathy using the packs of unopened and unmarked cards lying on the piano. Each of the performers made a modest bow when introduced. Maurel struck his pose for several seconds before bowing. It seemed more appropriate in this context.

They put on a remarkable display. Each performer in turn took a new pack of cards and proceeded through a rapid series of clever surprises. Cards tucked into one pocket would reappear in another. Cards picked at random by volunteers were identified by performers while blindfolded. Cards called out at random would miraculously appear at the top of a deck and so on. We were all delighted, and the laughter and applause grew steadily. The performers were extremely polished, Maurel not the least.

As a final round, each called up a volunteer and taught that person some new card trick in full view of all. Each volunteer managed to master his lesson after one or two tries until the room seemed filled by a warm congeniality between these masters and their fledgling audience.

One performer had a thick Italian accent and a charming old-world manner. Gently adjusting the hand and finger position of his volunteer, he might have resembled an elderly violin maestro in his conservatory or Verrochio guiding the brush of a very young DaVinci. I began to wonder about my own aversion to playing cards. In the hands of a kindly, well-meaning person, what harm could lie in these little pieces of cardboard?

Maurel took his turn last, deliberately, I suspect. He performed a routine whereby a specific card, eight of diamonds say, is inserted into the middle of the deck. The cards are shuffled several times, but that particular card invariably turns up on the bottom.

This is a simple feat achieved by always keeping an index finger on that card and moving it to the bottom as the rest of the deck is shuffled vigorously. It was described in several of the books I had seen, and I was surprised that Maurel had chosen such a simple trick, though his reason became all too clear a few minutes later.

When he selected a hand held up in the audience I saw that the volunteer who came forward was the fellow from Chicago whom I had met at last night's dinner. Maurel began by asking him if this was the first time he had seen this particular trick.

"No," the fellow said. "It's one that I do myself."

Maurel smiled with a look of mock surprise. "Would you care to demonstrate?" he asked, and slid the deck across the piano top toward his volunteer.

The fellow held up a card for all to see then allowed Maurel to reinsert it into the deck. Next, he shuffled the cards a few times on the draped piano and held up the deck so as to show the bottom card. There was a murmur of disappointment.

"Try again," said Maurel.

The fellow paused then repeated the process. Again the selected card failed to turn up on the bottom of the deck.

"If you please," said Maurel grandly, "I will demonstrate. Watch closely." He took the cards and went through the steps exactly as I had seen in the book, pausing at several points to show how his index finger never left contact with the subject card. He finished and pushed the deck over to his volunteer with a slight bow. I watched the fellow take a deep breath then repeat the steps just demonstrated. He failed again. There was some nervous laughter. A fourth and fifth attempt brought the same result. The audience began to shift uncomfortably.

Maurel seized the cards and ran through the routine rapidly, staring straight at the fellow who was quite flushed by now. There was a cold quality to Maurel's smile, and a truth suddenly hit me in the middle of my stomach.

Maurel was doing something to throw the trick off! He had lured this innocent fellow up before an audience and now was deliberately humiliating him. My discomfort turned to anger as I watched Maurel return the cards to the fellow then step back to wait, forcing his victim to try again. The silence was broken by voices here and there offering advice.

This time the fellow ran through the steps with his eyes closed, as if to call back some tactile memory he had lost. He failed again. Still Maurel did not move. What the devil was he trying to prove? His victim began another attempt but was interrupted when Maurel snatched away the cards and waved him off.

"Thank you, my friend," he said, "but you must leave these matters to us."

The fellow crept back to his seat. Maurel took a few steps away then stopped, weighing the deck in his palm.

"Something is missing," he said, and turned toward the piano, holding out his fingers as if feeling for heat or vibrations. "Ah!" he exclaimed, then stepped to the piano and threw back the tablecloth with a flourish.

"Here they are," he announced and picked up a handful of cards from the piano top to hold them above his head. As one might guess, they were the six or seven subject cards of the failed attempts. There was a general gasp then a burst of applause. Maurel flashed the cards to his right and left, snapping them open and shut with one hand like a lady's fan, then paraded them past the first row like a victory flag which prolonged the applause until he resumed his seat in triumph.

The proceedings closed, and people began the usual hubbub of rising and filing out. One of the first to leave was the man Maurel had so abused. He looked stricken. His wife was holding tightly to his arm, blinking back tears.

I left in angry confusion. Why had Maurel invited me to see such a display? As a reporter, it was my job to confront him and ask, but I didn't want to. There was something repellent about what I had just seen, the discomfiture of the victim, of course, but something else as well. And so I took a coward's way out by avoiding both Maurel and the couple from Chicago the rest of the afternoon.

I went to dinner early and sat at a different table. When a coterie of participants swept into the room together, Maurel among them, I wolfed down my meal and slipped out with a pocketful of cheese wedges.

That evening's event was held in a large ballroom on the floor above the mezzanine. Several hundred chairs had been set in rows and a stage had been erected at one end. Behind this were tall, floor-to-ceiling windows that looked out over the roof of the veranda toward the lake.

The program booklet announced this as a "Magical Masque," and in the operatic spirit of such an event we were all given paper masks of various colors that tied in back and covered the upper halves of our faces. Peering out through the eye holes, I thought we looked like an army of merry thieves gathering by lamplight for some devilish adventure. A row of kerosene footlights lined the front of the stage while the moon, nearly full, was visible through the windows behind. The combined effects made the entire ballroom seem unreal, like painted stage scenery, and when organ music arose from one corner

I thought Mephistopheles himself might rise up through the floor.

Mephistopheles did not arrive, but a troupe of magicians did. They processed down the center aisle in a slow lockstep, thirteen men in black formal dress, each wearing a brilliant, scarlet cape around his shoulders and a matching turban such as an Indian rajah might wear, and each of these bearing an enormous jewel at its front. Their faces were entirely shrouded in black hoods marked with odd letters and symbols in gold paint about the eyeholes.

They mounted the stage and faced us in a semi-circle. When their leader raised his arm, the music stopped. Then he chanted three distinct words from some language I couldn't identify, and the others repeated them in chorus. These turned out to be the only words spoken during the entire presentation, which must have lasted over an hour. It was like no other illusionist performance I had ever seen before or would ever see again.

The music resumed, strange Wagnerian chords that rose and sank one into the other. The performers moved about silently in rehearsed, sometimes symmetrical patterns, coming forward in pairs and quartets to carry out a seamless flow of difficult feats while others produced the necessary trunks, tables and other paraphernalia from behind screens at each side, moving back and forth in a formally sequenced manner like acolytes. When bringing objects to their leader, the others would often nod obsequiously and retreat without turning their backs to him.

Sparkling pitchers of water were brought forward in this ceremonial manner to be held aloft then lowered slowly into black bags where they simply evaporated. All manner of swords and spikes passed harmlessly through flesh. Four of the performers became rigid as corpses and were raised weightlessly overhead by comrades at head and foot who carried them about in a circular funeral procession around their leader in the center.

As I watched, it occurred to me that most of these feats had been seen in the theatres of Baltimore, and yet in this strangely choreographed, almost affected ritual they seemed totally new and hypnotic. The performers seemed to take no notice of the audience. The audience, in turn, seemed mesmerized and watched in frozen silence. When I glanced at those around me they seemed little more than a herd of masks with little, mole-like eyes, breathing softly and nodding at the completion of each feat. And as I continued to watch with them, I began to think, yes, this is new and hypnotic – new, hypnotic and somehow ominous and intimidating.

Now the performers had returned to their original semi-circle, this time joining hands. The music stopped. Once again, their leader chanted his mysterious three-word incantation. The others responded in antiphonal chorus. Then began a long, breathless silence. We waited. A few chairs creaked.

Suddenly, I heard someone gasp out loud. There was a muffled scream from somewhere at the back of the darkened hall. I leaned forward and saw that all thirteen men appeared to have risen several inches off the stage floor. I heard myself mutter "No" out loud. Then came a blinding flare-up of photographer's flash powder. When the smoke cleared, they were gone.

5

No doubt they simply had crawled under the back of the stage or perhaps slipped behind the screens and exited through the windows onto the veranda roof. I may have spent thirty seconds figuring this out when I noticed that I still hadn't moved from my seat. Most of the audience hadn't either. Applause had been tentative and short, as though out of place. People spoke in whispers, and it took us a good while to file out of the ballroom.

I stood in a corner and watched the others move off, many still wearing their paper masks. If creating a general sense of reverential awe was the intent of the performers, it certainly succeeded. I tore my mask in half and went down through the foyer and outside to clear my head.

The moon had drifted to the far end of the lake by now and seemed to have caught itself on the top of the stone tower. Odd things happen during full moons, I thought, and now it's nearly full. The whole day had put me off, first Maurel's behavior and now something about this arcane ceremony of a magic show.

I walked up and down the carriageway, kicking at the pebbles by the light of the veranda lanterns until an attendant came by to turn them down for the night. When I finally went up to bed, it took me a long time to fall asleep.

At breakfast, I learned that it had rained unexpectedly during the night, not a good sign for my plan, but good for washing away my mood of the night before. I skipped the first morning session in order to make the most of my last legitimate meal and pocketed more biscuits for one poor fish I had in mind.

When I had paid my hotel bill and turned in the room key I went out toward the waiting station wagon with my bag, which now resembled a picnic basket. Halfway there, I made a sharp detour to have a "last look" through the formal garden. Here was what appeared to be a white marble statue of an angel, about waist high, pouring water into a lily pond from an urn on her shoulder.

I waited until the two of us were alone, then darted behind the stables and up the hill into a pine forest. The wagon rolled off with a half-dozen passengers. I waited several long minutes, then hid my bag under some pine boughs and reentered the hotel through a service door.

One of the libraries had been turned into a classroom with rows of extra chairs, and the fellow with the Italian accent was teaching in an oversized bathrobe and pointed wizard's cap, apparently about the use of animals on stage. There was laughter at something he had just said as I slipped into a side seat. I noticed that the young girl who had been feeding the fish was seated next to her parents on the front row. Someone in the back row asked something.

"A gooda question," our teacher said. "I 'splain. No. – I showa you."

He darted behind the front table and produced a cardboard box painted to resemble a miniature barn. When he slid open its tiny door, we could see the yellow fluff of baby chicks. Then began the most charming little magic show I have ever witnessed.

"One-a, two-a, three-a baby cheeks," he said, snatching them out of the box into a line across the table. "Nine-a, ten-a, 'leven-a, twelve." And before the baby birds could so much as turn around, or we could count them to be sure, he held a scarf in front of them, snapped it once, and they were gone.

"Cheeks all-a gone," he said, and paused. "No wait. I hear." He cocked an ear, looked around him, then peered into one of his oversized sleeves. "How you get-a there?" he demanded and began to pull chicks from his sleeve, setting them on the table up to nine. We laughed and clapped. "They never tell-a me," he protested, and pulled one from each side pocket. A twelfth tumbled down when he lifted his wizard's cap.

Then he began a rapid sleight-of-hand, moving chicks from table to sleeve to box and back with a rhythmic count and commentary that had us giggling and clapping like children. (I recalled having felt this way years earlier with my older brothers, laughing hysterically and jumping from a loft into a wagon of new-mown hay.) We all were gasping for air when one of the baby birds tumbled from the table onto the carpet.

Quickly, the young girl jumped from her chair to pick it up and hold it against her face. At this, the magician clasped his hands together against his chest and froze. We all froze, charmed by the picture. Finally, he produced a small, lacquered box.

"We put-a heem een hees leetle house, eh?" He bent down, took the little bird carefully, closed it in the box and held it to her ear. "He there?"

She nodded. He straightened up, put it to his own ear, held it aloft a moment, then listened again. "I think he gone," he said and put it to the girl's ear again.

"Open it," she pleaded.

He did, and with a mock show of alarm, showed

us an empty box. He made a show of searching his sleeves and pockets, shook out his cap and was going through his props on the table when he suddenly stopped, put a finger to his temple and stared at the girl. Then he rushed over to her, put his hand into the large bow at the back of her dress and produced the chick. The girl jumped and clapped her hands. Our applause tumbled after.

Later, I sat alone at the far end of the card room with my pad and pencil, trying to capture the stark contrast between this little show and last night's spectacle. It was easy enough to write about what I had just seen, but my every attempt to get at the core of the other sounded exactly like the claptrap Wilson was sure to pencil out. I stared out the window at the huge granite boulders supporting the catwalk across the lake. Real, I thought, and perfectly captured in the word "rock." Perhaps my tentative sentences sounded like claptrap because it was claptrap that I was describing, impressive as it had seemed at the time.

That was it! And there was something more too. "Otis Elkerlick" was claptrap as well. So now I understood my discomfiture of the night before.

How had I come to this juncture? I started out as an imposter and had become a trespasser as well. Why couldn't I have used my real name? Why didn't I bring more money somehow? When I grow old, surely I will look back on all this as the worst folly of my life. I sat ruing in this vein for about an hour and finally decided to become myself again and go straight back to Baltimore where I belonged. I reached for the train ticket in my pocket but pulled out the program booklet instead. It was folded back to the page of that day's events. I stared mindlessly at it for a minute, then found that I was looking at the name "Zoromagus."

The general session Saturday afternoon was to be a symposium, and his name was at the end of a short list of speakers. I might go, I thought, whatever my misgivings. If these people were to speak openly about their craft, maybe I could write something convincing after all, or at least feel less like an outsider. Beside, it was to be in the ballroom. I could return to that troublesome spot and hear straight talk by the light of day.

It did look very different this time. The afternoon sun shimmered off the lake onto the walls and ceiling. The screens were gone from the stage, replaced by a lectern and a long, draped table with chairs for the speakers. This time there was no dramatic introit. The speakers drifted in one or two at a time like the audience. It felt a bit like required chapel or assembly at college. I saw Maurel and a few others I had noticed before enter together and take seats up front. The room filled up, the long table filled up, and we began.

First, the conference host in the cutaway (now with a big lily in his lapel) made a short speech congratulating himself and all present for such a fine attendance at the conference and urging everyone to come back and do it every year hereafter. (This confirmed Wilson's cynical observation about renting empty hotel rooms, of course.) Then came a string of laudatory introductions. Each speaker in turn made a polite bow to the applause, Signor this, Count that, and so on till finally Maestro Zoromagus rose. There was an extended ovation from Maurel and his claque.

Except for a large, waxed mustache and an enormous jeweled ring on one hand, there seemed nothing exceptional about the great Zoromagus that I could see. He appeared middle-aged, of average height, and looked about like the others in formal afternoon dress. Taking notes on the opening remarks of each speaker, I began to think of Maurel as a great fool for so revering this stage performer.

There was a short speech on the difficulty of illusion as an art form and the need for years of solitary practice, then another on the importance of developing an original style. I don't recall most of the others (and no longer have my notes, as I will explain later) except for one speaker's impassioned diatribe on the important distinction between illusion and magic.

Illusion, he explained, was a fine art, like painting or music, created to please and to lift the spirit. Magic, on the other hand, was sinister and irreligious, drawn from dark and inhuman forces to be totally avoided by all right-thinking people. Coming from a lectern this sounded pretty much like a Sunday sermon.

It was some time during this speech that I began to sense that from his chair, Zoromagus was staring, glowering rather, in my direction.

This man was unknown to me, and surely I was unknown to him. But under his clearly malevolent gaze I sensed that he was on to me somehow. Perhaps he suspected me as a potential detractor, or worse, a trespassing stowaway and a fraud. I looked away then back again, but Zoromagus had not shifted his glare. All that Maurel had said of him now seemed true, his clairvoyant perception, his hypnotic gaze, his intimidating presence. When he finally rose to speak, he bypassed the lectern and came to the edge of the stage without breaking his gaze so that he appeared to be coming straight down on me.

By now I had stopped breathing. At that moment, it was as if the two of us were entirely alone, fifty feet apart in that cavernous room. Zoromagus raised his fist above his head and shouted.

"Liar! Impostor! Devil!"

I stiffened. This was the voice of the mysterious incantation the night before.

"You bring everything destructive and evil into this place," he bellowed. "I will not have you destroy all that we have built here. Leave at once! Go! Go now!"

He brought his fist down like a hammer, one finger pointing straight at me.

"You!"

There were gasps. I started to rise, but my legs were powerless. I thought I might faint. I started to pull myself up by the chair in front of me but felt a hand on my shoulder from the back. I sank into my chair, relieved not to have fallen.

There was whispering and muttering all about now, but none of it seemed focused right on me. People ahead were turning around in their seats to look. I turned too and saw others half rising to let someone pass down the row behind me and move slowly toward the exit and out. It was the old, bearded fellow in the rumpled suit who had given up his seat in the wagon down at the train depot two days earlier.

6

For the rest of the session I tried to be invisible in my seat. Zoromagus apologized smoothly for the disruption, but I wondered if it all hadn't been prearranged. He launched into an eloquent little sermon about how the gift of illusionist skill was a trust and easily abused in the wrong hands. The old man may have been such a miscreant, though he didn't say so directly. I was taking copious notes by now.

Let me pause a minute to say that, here, in the second half of the twentieth century I am struck by how much the art of public speaking has changed in my lifetime. The introduction of the microphone and electric loudspeaker has eliminated the need to bellow and use broad theatrical gestures for emphasis. And with the demise of roaring and posturing, the taste for florid rhetoric has passed as well.

Zoromagus was striding about the stage with much pausing and posing for effect. He was saying that we were a very select group, entrusted with secrets that set us apart from the unskilled. These secrets were never to be revealed to the general public. If so, the illusionist's art would become ordinary and surely come to be held in contempt. There were nods and murmurs of agreement around me.

"We are the chosen," he said, bringing his arms down from above his head and spreading them out wide. "Moreover, we must be honest with ourselves and recognize that within our select group there are distinct levels of skill and insight – tiers, if you will."

I had a vague sense that he was leading us down some path. Coming up here in the wagon, Maurel had intimated that this fellow had played a part in setting up this whole conference.

"Each tier, and there are many," he continued, "represents a level of skill founded upon knowledge of a body of secrets. We must accept the fact that most who practice our art cannot climb beyond a lower tier, and for these good souls the secrets of the next tier must always remain — you will forgive my expression," and here he smiled with a little bow, "above their heads."

So that's it, I thought. According to this dogma, Antoine Junius Maurel, the disciple, was simply claiming his tier in front of the press when he knocked that poor fellow from Chicago off his ledge. I was scribbling furiously by now.

But the great Zoromagus was not done. He went to a window at the rear of the stage and pointed to the distant cliff side with its rising pathway dotted with gazebos. "Our art is mastered so," he said, "by a long and arduous climb during which most stop at one of the resting places and go no further while others, the few, may reach the foot of that tower. Perhaps even climb the stairs." He turned to the other speakers now and made another of his little bows. It occurred to me that Maurel had adopted this mannerism.

"And in the tower," pausing here, "well, dear friends, we must have order. Order and direction. The world of illusion will soon become a refuge for quackery and witchcraft unless we can establish trusted and knowledgeable leadership to set standards. We must have an authority able to separate true illusionists from those who are false. A winnowing of wheat from the chaff. A purifying, if you will."

"Pope Zoromagus the First" I wrote across my pad and snapped it shut.

Over the next several minutes he proposed an elaborate hierarchy for illusionists. There were to be titled ranks and officers, secret synods and trial councils to "expose" those practitioners who brought a shadow over the illusionist's art by calling up the dark powers of superstition and witchcraft. His theatrical skill surprised and annoyed me. At one point he explained how those of higher rank were obligated to lead and control those below, coming down the stage steps to speak from the aisle as he said this.

"We would have no socialist union," he assured us, "but a guild, a legion of like-minded performers similar to the Meistersinger jury of recent operatic fame or perhaps even an secret order such as the medieval Knights Templar."

I had never been to an opera at that time, let alone Wagner's Die Meistersinger, but I had read Scott's Ivanhoe as a boy and knew something of the celibate Knights Templar and their religious crusades. Even so, all this was beginning to sound more like the Ku Klux Klan to my ear. Zoromagus ended with a bombastic flourish, referring to the Almighty in high purple and something that sounded like a doomsday threat from the Book of Revelation. Maurel and his claque jumped to their feet for a standing ovation. When most of the audience did as well, I slid down my row and ducked out.

I wanted to find the old fellow who had been sent away. It seemed that either he was merely what the rounders in my day called a "shill" or else he was the other half of my deathless, unwritten article. But I was stymied here. I didn't know his name, and even if I did, I couldn't ask about him at the hotel desk without making my presence known. I wandered out onto the veranda and was puzzling over how to find him when I felt a hand on my shoulder a second time and turned to discover that the old fellow had found me first.

He was smiling calmly, but I must have looked a little surprised, partly because he seemed to know that I wanted to see him and partly because of his size. He barely came up to my shoulder and probably had to stretch a bit to tap me there. Now he nodded at one of the small veranda tables where he must have been sitting. It had a white tablecloth with a pitcher of water and two long-stemmed glasses.

"I'm sorry," I said. "You must be waiting for someone."

"Always," he replied, "but you're here now."

We sat down together. Fumbling for words, I blurted out "I thought he meant me back there."

"I know," he said. "You started to get up. Why?"

"He was pointing right at me," I said.

"Or through you. He called me a liar and an imposter. Do you answer to those names?" He poured water into the glasses, still smiling.

"No," I said. "I'm Otis Elkerlick of the Baltimore Evening News."

But I felt myself caught the moment I said it. Then somehow aware of my dilemma, he put down the pitcher and held out his hand.

"My name is Janos," he said. (He pronounced it "Yanos.") "Janos Ferency." We shook hands.

"I saw you back at the station," I said. "I should have thanked you."

He shrugged.

"It's a long walk," I added. For some reason I couldn't find the words to ask what all this was about, so I sat staring at him.

He was clearly old, approaching eighty I guessed, with deep creases in his face. He had a beak nose and ears that seemed too large for his head. His sunburned scalp was visible through his gray hair that flared out in random strands. His beard had not been trimmed for some time so that it completely concealed his collar, if he wore one at all. It was difficult to guess what might have been the original color of his suit. His eyes, which he had not taken off me since we sat down, were dark and large. They reminded me of some I had seen in old paintings.

But now those eyes were looking past me rather than at me. His mouth had opened in a wide smile, revealing teeth brown, broken, or missing altogether. I turned to see what he was looking at.

It was Zoromagus bearing down on us from the hotel door. He had an entourage of six or eight young men in his wake, Maurel among them.

"So! The devil has found the press," Zoromagus roared. A few people nearby turned to look. "What fantastic libel has been invented now?"

Without waiting for an answer, he turned to me

with another of his little bows and a sudden flash of smile. He extended his hand with the large ring.

"I am Zoromagus, illusionist," he said. "You were in the hall this afternoon I believe, yes? My young friend here" (he nodded at Maurel) "tells me you are with the newspapers in Baltimore. You are a reviewer, a theatre critic, no?"

"Otis Elkerlick of the Baltimore Evening Sun," I said, barely getting it out. "Just a reporter. I believe I'm the only one here."

I had risen out of courtesy since he seemed intent on addressing just me. He pressed his ringed hand against his chest as if he were still speaking from a stage. I felt uncomfortable standing there in conversation with all his companions standing about like courtiers, and there was a funny rhythm to his speech that I hadn't noticed when he was on stage, though not what you'd call an accent. As he spoke, his eyes were shifting between me and the old fellow who hadn't moved from his seat.

"We must meet to talk in better company, eh?" he said. "You can come to our table for lunch tomorrow. You have many questions, I am sure."

The dining hall was off limits for me now, but before I could think of a smooth counter-suggestion, he pointed at the water glasses on our table.

"And here you are offered no more than water

when you have come to taste art." He lifted a glass of water by its stem, held it up against the light coming off the lake surface and turned it slowly between his fingers. "A poor draught for a guest in search of deep mysteries," he said, "yet transparent. Much like the motives of an old derelict charlatan. Allow me." He passed his right hand over the glass, covering the front of it with his draped fingers. "I believe we have all read of this one," he joked to the group at large. "I assure you, it is nothing." He pulled his hand away with a flourish and held the glass out for all to see. The water was now a dark wine red.

I had seen directions for this trick. It's done with powder held between the fingers or ink concealed in a ring. The real art lies in one's ability to distract the observer's gaze with hand motion, eye contact, or some seemingly artless comment tossed aside. This requires a level of skill I had not acquired, and while I understood what must have been done, it was stunning to see it executed so convincingly just a yard in front of my nose.

Now all eyes were on the old fellow as Zoromagus placed the glass in front of him and took a step back, smiling grimly. For a few seconds we all were rigid, poised as a cocked hammer. Then the old fellow, looking Zoromagus straight in the eye, made a slight gesture, brushing the back of his hand against the glass and knocking it over, as if by accident. The contents spilled out across the white tablecloth toward Zoromagus.

But now it was plain water again, crystal clear as the moment it had first been poured! I heard gasps. Zoromagus was opening and shutting his mouth, making no audible words. Finally, he spat one out.

"Devil!" He spun on his heel and walked away abruptly. His companions followed, a few looking back at the colorless puddle soaking into the white tablecloth. I thought I saw Maurel catch my eye and make a motion with his head as if to say – come with us. I turned to the old man. He was staring thoughtfully at what he had just done.

"Forgive my anger," he said softly, then turning to me added, "I need to be alone for a while. May we talk later?"

"Yes," I said. "Of course."

I watched him leave the veranda by the side steps and disappear around the corner of the hotel.

7

To say I was dumbfounded again would be an understatement. I had been in this place less than two full days but was beginning to feel totally off my feet. The dozens of magic shows I had seen in Baltimore and the simple sleight-of-hand I had practiced were no preparation for tumbling so deeply into this world of illusion. "Otis Elkerlick" was a fiction, and perhaps this hotel, this lake, these people and their mysterious feud were all some sort of dreamlike concoction that would pass when I returned to the real world.

Alone now, I stood by the table in a daze. Sunlight was shimmering on the lake surface. That's not real light, I thought. It's the illusion of light. Or possibly the light comes from beneath the surface from the real world. Everything here is just a reflection. I thought of Plato at college and how I had labored through his Allegory of the Cave in Greek. I had cheated, using a pony translation. I am not real either, I thought to myself. Was Plato? I noticed that I seemed to feel no contact with the table where my fingers were pressing down. There was no ground beneath the soles of my shoes. I didn't feel those either. And now the table was floating away.

It was a busboy removing the wet tablecloth.

"Finished Sir?" he asked.

"Yes. Thank you." I heard my own voice out loud and took a thumping step forward, testing the solid world, so to speak. I decided to sit down somewhere else and work on my notes. Writing had always helped.

At a corner desk in one of the libraries I opened my pad to a clean page and wrote T-O-M across the top as I had done in the first grade. Then I flipped the pages back to my notes and stared at my adult reporter's scrawl. Minutes later, I began to read, correcting mistakes and completing half-expressed observations. My own rational thoughts began to echo in my head again. When I looked up, an hour had passed and I was hungry.

"Dinner time", I clucked to myself. "Time to head for the woods." But stepping into the corridor, I ran smack into Maurel. He was in formal evening dress for the banquet.

"I've been looking for you," he said. "You weren't in your room."

"Obviously not," I said. I couldn't tell him I

had checked out.

He looked at my clothes. "You're not dressed yet. Where are you sitting?"

"I'm not going," I said. "I have some writing to do."

This seemed to bother him, and he was thoughtful for a moment. "We need to talk," he said somberly, "but this isn't a good place."

I nodded toward the end of the hall, and we walked down to the card and chess room. The young girl was there, teaching checkers to a much smaller boy. We stepped over toward the card tables.

"I'm worried about you, my friend," he began. "No telling what cock-and-bull he's told you."

"You mean Ferency?"

"Who?"

"Janos Ferency. The old man," I said.

"Is that his name now?" Maurel asked. "My God, he's had hundreds. What did you talk about?"

"Nothing," I said. "You came up just when we sat down. Is there some big secret?"

"No. It's just not a good idea for you to be around him. He can be very misleading."

"How so?" I asked.

Maurel bit his lip. He seemed very earnest and had dropped much of his theatrical manner.

"My friend," he said, "do you know much about madness?" He seemed to hiss the word.

"Madness?" I said out loud. "You mean insanity?"

The two children looked over at us curiously.

"Down this way," he said, motioning.

I followed him down the steps into the billiard parlor. It was deserted, and the lamps above each table had not been lit. When we stood between the tables in the gloom, Maurel's face, white tie and shirtfront seemed to be floating in space. His head was explaining something to the effect that a group of right-minded men were trying to organize a means of preventing devilry and superstition from creeping in and coloring public perception of the illusionist's art.

"Since when is that an issue?" I asked. "I've never noticed it."

"You've seen it yourself," the floating head answered. "You were there today."

"The old fellow? " I asked. "You're telling me he's some sort of threat?"

"He and those like him. They contaminate the profession."

My eyes were beginning to adjust – and my perspective as well. There was something naïve, almost boyish about Maurel's intensity.

"How can an obviously poor old man or even a hundred like him hurt you or your career in the least?" I demanded.

"By witchcraft," he answered.

"Witchcraft?" I snorted. "First it's madness and now witchcraft. Is it going to be voodoo and black magic too?" I heard myself speaking in the dark, the rational skeptic, the voice of Wilson and the Baltimore Evening News. But I had not forgotten my confusion of an hour before.

"Call it what you will," said Maurel. "When witchcraft and the art of illusion are practiced openly and side by side the world will make no distinction between them."

"All right," I said, "but what about that performance last night with the masks and all that ceremonial hokum or whatever it was? Wasn't the idea to make the audience believe it was actual magic?"

"The illusion of magic," he corrected. "It's done by art."

"Then what's the difference," I said. "If you're so worried about the general perception, why do all that spooky stuff?"

"It's what they want," he answered. "They crave magic, something that appears all-powerful. But they don't want devils."

"They could turn to religious faith," I said.

He shrugged. "They prefer miracles."

We were silent a moment. Finally I said, "It doesn't have to be that way. There was a perfectly charming show this morning. That little girl upstairs was delighted. We all were." I described the Italian fellow's demonstration with the baby chicks. "There was nothing ominous and dark about that," I said. "Why does it have to be intimidating?"

"That's old Torelli," Maurel said. "Did he do the chick-in-the-box finish?"

"Yes," I said. "It turned up in the bow of her dress."

"A different chick," he snapped. "The box has a false bottom on a spring. The bird in the box is simply crushed flat."

I remembered the girl holding the chick, that chick against her face. Then I imagined Torelli later, cleaning a pathetic little mess out of his box.

"That's very cruel," I said.

"Think of it as a sacrifice," he replied.

"Sacrifice to what?"

"To the illusion, of course," he answered.

It wasn't making much sense. He seemed to be going in a circle. I had a sudden thought that this was only a performance, and Maurel was leading me around in some sort of false logic like the numbers tricks I had seen the day before or the knots that weren't really knots at all. He was rattling on in this strange manner when I interrupted.

"What's between Zoromagus and the old fellow anyway," I asked. "It's obviously pretty bitter."

"Of course," he said. "He's exactly what I'm talking about. He follows Zoromagus around the world, even up here, just to upstage him."

"With real magic, you're saying."

"Black magic," he said. "The old man's a warlock and a sorcerer. Do you doubt such things?"

"I don't doubt upstaging," I said.

So maybe that's it, I thought. The rag-tag old fellow isn't a real threat but just a stalking horse. And this guild or whatever would be able to discredit any competitor they chose, Harry Houdini for example. The likely prize could be more or better bookings. Maurel, the disciple, would get his share. The St. Louis Exposition would be coming up in 1904. Did they have their eyes on that?

"Look," I said finally. "I have no intention of getting into any of this or even writing about it. It could be libel and my editor would cut it anyway." (I couldn't bring myself to say, "If he prints anything I write at all.") "I'm going to submit a straight description of the events here. Who, what, where, when. That's all. I'm a reporter, not an inquisitor. All right?"

Maurel shrugged and made a dismissive gesture, the same with which he had sent away the poor fellow whose card trick he had sabotaged.

"I must go," he said. "I've been asked to propose a toast tonight." (I could guess to whom or what.) He was starting up the stairs but turned. "If you have a chance to mention any names . . .," he was saying.

"I'll mention yours," I said.

He struck his stage pose. "I'd be most grateful." He started up again but turned a second time. "Do have lunch with us tomorrow, and . . . keep clear of Ferency or whatever he calls himself now. He's trouble." And then as he ran up, he tossed back, "Besides, he's a Jew."

8

I'm not sure how long I stayed alone in that dim room. Everyone else would be heading for the dining hall by now, and down here seemed as good a place as any to remain unnoticed. Billiards was foreign to me, though a schoolmate had once explained it with a pencil and little wads of paper. Young people today are likely to confuse it with pool or what was sometimes called "pocket billiards." True billiards, the gentleman's game, is played on a pocketless table with a white ball and two or three red balls. (I forget which.) You score points or whatever by the way you make contact between the balls, bouncing them off the sides, hitting more than one at a time and so on.

I was as ignorant of the fine points then as I am today. Nonetheless, I took down a cue and tried my hand in the fading light. Here is what I found.

The cue is like a force of some sort, say an urge or an idea. It strikes a person who is somehow destined to be hit by that urge or idea because he's different from his fellows, like a white ball among red ones. The power of his idea sends him scurrying off to tell a friend, convert him, if you will. He wants company to travel along with him in his same direction.

But there's a problem. That cue force might have hit him just a mite off center. Maybe his head was turned a little or something. Anyway, he goes running off to tell this idea to his friend, the red ball, only he, the white ball, is a bit off line and doesn't know it. They click together and everything sounds good, but when the red ball goes off to find another friend, or his own convert let's call it, he's a little more off line than his teacher, the white ball, was.

So this red ball hits another red ball even more off center, and now this third fellow goes off on a route that has almost nothing to do with the original direction of the cue. You wouldn't know it's the same idea. But if there's enough force behind it, that last ball will run into some hard part of the world and come careening off back at the first ball, that white one. They'll knock heads – hard, then back apart and glare, like enemies, red ball and white ball. They won't even recognize each other.

It had been several hours since I had eaten anything, and I felt ravenous. In the main lobby a different clerk was on duty and barely glanced up as I passed through. Behind the hotel, my bag was just as I had left it, and I ate the better part of my precious store all at once.

After, I lay on my back to watch the sky through the pine branches overhead. They moved slightly in the breeze, changing the shapes of the open patches. There was a reddish tinge to the light now, and it made the boughs look black, like arms in formal coat sleeves. When I closed my eyes there were men making grand stage gestures and pulling things out of boxes and people's pockets. Eventually, they seemed to be waving and beckoning to me while I seemed to be floating and slipping further and further away.

Then, somehow, I was submitting my article to Wilson who sat on the porch swing of my home in Ohio. When I tried to read it aloud, I couldn't see the words.

"It's in Latin," I said, "to protect the secrets." I wanted to prove it by showing him my Cicero text where I had cribbed it, but I had left that book on the train from Baltimore. When I went back to search, Maurel turned up, claiming it had been in the hotel library the whole time. I found it in my old college library instead, but now it was a copy of the New York World. Someone had used it to wrap the crushed and bloody body of some small animal, but its little black eyes were still alive and blinking. There was a huge headline in two-inch letters that seemed to be speaking out loud from inside my head.

"The little girl is crushed," I heard myself say. Then I was trying to squeeze myself down to show what that meant.

When I awoke, it was night and chilly. I had slid down the hill a yard or so, and there were pine needles up the back of my jacket. I shook myself out, found my derby, and discovered that I was thirsty as a camel.

"Time to drop in at the stone angel," I said aloud to perk myself up.

There was a full moon that night, and I would have been quite visible from the windows on the formal garden side of the hotel, but there were no lamps burning behind them. It must have been very late. At the garden lily pond I had to weave through shrubbery and approach the marble statue from the rear, then kneel and hold onto the back of her head with one hand while I stretched my cupped hand out under the stream of water. (I wasn't about to use my new hat.) It took a long time to get my fill that way. When my hand went numb from the cold water I dried it on my trousers and slid it inside my shirt to get the feeling back.

"Here I am," I thought, clinging to an angel in the middle of the night with my hand on my heart. We must make a dramatic picture together. But when I stood up and looked down at the figure in the moonlight, I saw that it wasn't an angel at all but just a female figure in a flowing robe that suggested wings. It seemed to have changed right under my hand – and while I was wide awake. Slight as this was, it sent a peculiar chill through me.

I decided to walk it off and began to march up and down the garden paths, swinging my arms and focusing intently on all that was visible in the moonlight. That's peony, that's rhododendron, now laurel, privet over there and so on. Here at the back were large open bins, one of compost, another of gravel. And well behind these, a stack of wooden beehives. Honey for the dining guests, no doubt. I halted before a large brown rabbit sitting in my path. We eyed each other. I held out my derby.

"Sorry," I said. "Can't fit you in here."

Across the carriageway from the garden were the veranda stairs where I had first entered the hotel. These were supported by a pair of rustic arches. Going through them took one under the veranda into a dark, cavernous space that served as the boathouse. Here were wooden walkways separated by the open water of the boat slips. No moonlight penetrated here, but I knew there was an opening at the front where the docks began, where I had seen the young girl feeding the fish.

I entered and felt my way along the planks step by step, running my hand over the polished sides of the wooden canoes that lay inverted on their racks.

There was a slight smell of fish in the air. It mixed with the odor of wet wood and tar, and as I crept along, I became aware for the first time of an ongoing chorus of frogs and insects.

At the front doorway where the docks began, I passed from near total darkness into bright moonlight. Here I froze in my tracks. The lake and its cliffside borders had been a lovely landscape by day. Now, by night, it seemed to have turned into an interior space of colossal gothic proportions, a cathedral nave with stone walls towering overhead, an immense open floor like black obsidian, and a length beyond any archbishop's grandest dream. It made me dizzy.

I stood still, taking this in for the better part of a minute before my eyes focused down and right ahead of me on the central dock. What I saw startled me again. Ferency, the old fellow, was seated on a stack of wooden planks, apparently intended for dock repairs. He was staring out toward the far end of the lake, seemingly unaware of me. In those days my eyes were better than they are now, and I recall vividly how his age seemed altered by the moonlight. The lines on his face had disappeared like the wrinkles of his worn suit, and his gray hair and beard looked a pale blond. His folded hands rested on one knee thrown over the other. Composed in this fashion he might have been seated in some gilded and velvet opera house taking in a concert. "The music of the spheres," I thought.

My first resonant footstep out onto the dock broke the spell.

He looked toward me and smiled, pointing to a space beside him on the stacked lumber. As I walked toward him a breeze blew across the water, and I felt as though I were stepping out over an open canyon. My shoes made a soft drumbeat on the planks.

"Good evening, my friend," he said as I came up. "What brings you out at this hour?"

"I was thirsty," I replied. My answer made little sense, but he seemed to understand what I meant.

"And you?" I asked, taking a seat beside him. I had a sudden notion that he, too, was without a hotel room, perhaps had been without one since we arrived.

"I come to find peace," he said. "Anger is never the answer."

"You had good reason," I said.

He shook his head. "No. I knew perfectly well what he would do."

"I gather that you two know each other," I said. It was a stupid thing to say, but he didn't seem to mind.

"True," he agreed. "Many years." Then turning to me, he said, "Tell me of you."

I began to explain my connection to the Baltimore Evening News and about the article I intended to write. He started to smile again as if I were retelling an old, familiar joke.

"No, no," he said. "I meant about you. Why are you interested in magic, you yourself?"

I hadn't told him that I was. He simply knew. At that moment I had intended to say how it brought pleasure to people and taught us to observe more closely, that it could be regarded as an art, like painting or music as I had heard explained in a lecture that afternoon. But I said none of those things.

Perhaps it was the intimidating effect of feeling small and exposed out in the middle of that cavernous space with moonlight beaming down on me, or else the comfort of a kindly presence sharing my shelterless state, or both, but after a moment I heard myself say something I had hardly dared to think before.

"It's the power," I said. "I love the feeling of power. It makes me feel – superior."

It felt like I had confessed a crime. I wanted to say how terrible it was, that I knew it was arrogant foolishness, that I wasn't who I claimed to be, perhaps never had been. But I said none of these things either. After a moment, I felt his hand on my shoulder for a third time.

"It's perfectly natural, Thomas," he said. "Perfectly natural."

I could have fallen through the dock into the lake. He had called me out by my real name! And suddenly I thought I might burst into tears for the first time since a schoolyard fight in the sixth grade.

I didn't burst into tears, but I came pretty well uncorked as it was. For what seemed like an hour, I poured out the trivial details of my young life: Ohio, family, school, friends, college, the discarded prospect of the ministry, my recent months in Baltimore. Brutally honest as I tried to be, his rapt interest gave me a sense that the most ordinary detail was enormously important, and that somehow or other I was too. I was describing my inbred prejudice against playing cards and half mocking myself when he interrupted me.

"If you feel that way, why do you carry them with you?" he asked.

"I don't," I said. But I searched my pockets anyway and found an unopened box of hotel cards in the right hip pocket of my trousers, the side opposite him.

"Sorry," I said. "I didn't know."

"Nothing to be sorry for," he said. "You couldn't have known."

His meaning was clear, but how he put them there was inexplicable. We were sitting two feet apart, and he had touched me only on my left shoulder. I thought of Maurel and his warning in the billiard room.

"May I ask about you?" I said.

"Certainly, my friend." He shifted around to face me directly, as if to welcome all questions.

"You are a magician, of course," I began, then corrected myself. "An illusionist, that is."

"'Magician' is fair enough," he said.

"Where do you perform?" I asked.

"Here, there, the world over," he said. "To be truthful, in recent years it's been almost entirely in tight spots."

For a moment I wondered if he meant his apparent poverty or else some sort of escape artistry. Then fumbling around for a smooth way to ask a tough question I finally said, "I understand what professional rivalry means and how bitter competition can be, but you were called some rather nasty names today."

"You mean 'devil' and 'liar'? 'Charlatan' too, I believe."

"Yes," I said. "And I was told some other things too."

"Such as?" He seemed amused.

I wanted to ask about black magic, about witchcraft, but there seemed no tactful way to get the words together. The whole topic seemed rude and ridiculous. I felt uncomfortably warm in my jacket, despite the breeze, and something was pressing in on my temples.

"There was a fellow here," I started. "I mean, I guess he's still here . . . ," I broke off.

"One of the ones who came over to our table

today?" he suggested.

"Yes," I said.

"Well then," he said, "what did he tell you?"

"Oh, just a bucket of stuff. Foolish stuff." I felt myself backing down.

"Did you argue?"

"No. Not really," I answered.

There was a pause. I had brought this up on my own, and now it was going nowhere while I just fumbled with my hat in my hands.

He spoke softly. "Tell me what you need to say, my friend."

I had been facing out across the water. When I turned to look at him, it seemed that he had never taken his eyes off me and was still smiling his calm smile.

"He told me you practice black magic," I said. "You know, real magic, supernatural. Not illusion." I thought I heard myself speaking too fast, too loudly.

"Such things have been said before," he said, nodding.

I spoke slowly and softly now. "And he called you a warlock and a sorcerer."

He smiled again, this time with a slight shrug.

"What do you think?" he asked. "Who do you say I am?"

It was the perfect moment for that very question. Almost every event since my arrival had been leading me toward this, the constant surprises, the unexplainable tricks, the self-seeking ambition and jealousy of some, and finally the bitter and seemingly unjust ridicule of this wise and gentle person with powers apparently beyond the others. Under other circumstances I never would have had the inspiration to penetrate such a disguise or found the audacity to identify him by name to his face, but at that moment I felt those strengths welling up in me. I looked straight into his eyes and spoke.

"You are – Harry Houdini," I said.

He blinked. I saw that he was trying to suppress a laugh. Finally, he let out a delighted howl, showing the stubs of his bad teeth.

It had happened again. My senses and experience had told me one thing, but a twist of the kaleidoscope made it something else. Now I was laughing too, at first in embarrassment, then at the absurdity of my suggestion.

"Houdini is a very young man," he said between gasps, "just a few years older than you. Besides, I believe he's in Europe now."

And then I remembered having read something to that effect in a recent newspaper and felt all the sillier for my conviction just seconds earlier. But laughter is surely a great tonic, for I felt drawn to this old fellow and sensed that here, with only the night as our witness, we had formed a bond, an unspoken pact to shed all pretense. So when my newfound friend suggested that we take a walk around the lake, I agreed.

"We can discuss anything you wish," he said, and began to take off his shoes.

"Why are you doing that," I asked.

He held up a shoe for my inspection. "To save my sole," he said spookily, then burst into giggles and added, "I'm used to traveling this way." His feet were small and calloused. He wore no socks.

Thus, we set off together down the dock toward the shore and into the night, he with his old shoes under one arm and I with my new derby back on my head. But the lake must have been a sounding board amplifying our glee, for when I glanced up at the hotel I saw a figure on an upper balcony turn quickly and slip back inside.

9

We emerged from the boathouse on the opposite side from where I had entered earlier and started up the footpath toward the far end of the lake. This followed the shore briefly then angled off a few yards into the trees to begin a long, gentle ascent to where moonlight showed the tower as a tarnished silver column against black sky. The path allowed us to walk side by side. It was dirt, hard-packed around broken rock and small pebbles, but my barefoot companion didn't seem bothered.

"This was all ice eons ago," he said waving his free hand out toward the lake gorge. "When the glaciers receded it was like the earth had been scored by the fingers of God. Ever read Aggasiz? Humboldt?"

I said I hadn't.

"Good men," he said. "Traveled all over God's creation. Wrote down what it told them."

His mention of religion and science in one

breath intrigued me. "Tell me about you," I said. "Where are you from?"

"Lately or originally?" he asked.

"Start with originally and work up to lately," I replied.

He laughed. "Born in Egypt," he said.

"Egypt?"

"Parents were traveling at the time," he said. "Actually, they were traveling all the time. They were performers, magicians mostly, both of them, wandering around from market to opera house to palace and back, all over Europe and the East, following their star, like magi."

"On camels too?" I joked.

"Only when necessary," he said. "Damn things have fleas. Anyway, that was my education."

"You've been a magician all your life then," I said.

He went on. "More often a teacher, I'd say. Advisor for those too proud to be taught. Doctor and friend to the wisest. I did as my parents did before me."

"Where did you do this," I asked.

"Oh my." He paused and thought. "Moscow, Madrid, Alexandria, and on and on again over the horizon."

I remembered what Maurel had told me riding up to the hotel in the station wagon. "It sounds a bit like what I was told about Zoromagus," I said.

He was silent for several moments. I listened to our footsteps, mine thumping, his padding. There was a rise and fall of breeze through the pines.

"What you were told about Zoromagus is absolutely true," he said softly. "He did every bit of it."

"Don't count on it," I said. "I know for a fact that some of the things I heard had to happen over half a century ago. Zoromagus couldn't be much over fifty himself."

"Forty-seven, to be exact," he said, "but it's true all the same."

"I don't understand," I said.

We walked some more in silence. Finally, he said, "He didn't do those things. I did them."

"You?"

He nodded.

"Then how can you say Zoromagus did them?" I asked.

He stopped on the path and turned to face me. "Because he isn't really Zoromagus," he said. "I am."

The memory of Maurel hissing the word "madness" flashed through my mind. I felt heartsick. The old fellow must have read it on my face, because he smiled.

"Don't worry," he said. "I'm no lunatic. It would have been better to say I was Zoromagus. And by right, still am."

I might have stood there all night with my jaw hanging open if he hadn't said, "Come along. I'll explain as we go."

And as we continued up the mountain path, it seemed to me that the higher we went, the more I got down to the bottom of things.

"Zoromagus was a stage name my father concocted," he said. "Actually, it was my mother's idea. She had the imagination. Did most of his talking too. They became Zoromagus together, so to speak. Anyway, they were Hungarian, you might guess, but 'Zoromagus' was mysterious, powerful sounding. 'Magus' means wise. Has a Biblical ring to it. Ever read the Bible?"

I laughed without bothering to answer.

"The 'Zoro' is Zoroaster, of course, with all that business about light and darkness. Put together, it sounds good, even if it doesn't mean much. Invented to impress people, that's all. Sort of like your little nom-de-plume."

I winced and heard him chuckle.

"Anyway, it's memorable," he continued. "I learned their trade and then some. I was still a boy, not even your age, and one day . . ." (he waved his hand as if dismissing something) "they were gone."

"What happened?" I asked.

"Typhoid," he said. "There's black magic for

you. Makes whole lives disappear. Families. Villages."

"I'm sorry," I said. There had been grim accounts in the papers, and this was just a few years before the famous Typhoid Mary case right there in New York State. My friend went on.

"They had nothing to leave me, so I helped myself to the name. I became Zoromagus. That's when I really began to understand magic. I learned what my parents probably knew all along."

"Which was?"

He held up one finger. "There's magic in a name, Thomas. Real magic. It gives us the courage to do things we wouldn't dare otherwise. It can change you into a different person." He paused. "Of course, that person can be either an angel or a devil."

"Or just a fool," I added.

"Don't be so hard on yourself, my young friend," he said.

"So how did this Zoromagus here come by the name?" I asked. "Did he just appropriate it? He seems arrogant enough."

When he didn't answer right off, I felt as if I had stepped over a line. We were about halfway to the far end of the lake now and coming up on one of the resting places, a small gazebo of cedar poles and shingles. It sat out on a rock ledge away from the trees to allow a view of the lake and the hotel behind us. We stopped beside it.

"I mean, who was he before?" I said.

He entered the gazebo and I followed. We sat facing each other, my shoe tips nearly touching his bare toes. The moon had traveled a good bit by now, putting the old man in silhouette. I watched the strands of his hair tremble in the breeze. I'd gone too far to back out, but it seemed hard to get my words together.

I said, "Was he . . . I mean, is he – your son?" I was leaning forward, afraid to miss his answer.

"No," he said finally, "not exactly. I found him in Liverpool. Eleven years old and sleeping in a barrel, a runaway from some church orphanage. They beat him for stuttering. Could hardly speak at all. I took him with me. Gave him food and better clothes. And eventually speech."

I sat back. So that explained the funny speech rhythm when he came up to our table that afternoon.

"He speaks beautifully on stage," I said.

"He has great faith in his own words," was the reply.

"You can take some credit for that," I offered. It was meant as a compliment, but I saw his shoulders sag. After a moment, he picked up his shoes and stood.

"We aren't there yet," he said.

It wasn't clear if he meant to some place or to

the end of his story, but I followed.

The end of the lake was almost half a mile further, and we must have covered most of that before he spoke again. I sensed that he had been working up to saying something more.

"Once people started calling me 'Zoromagus'," he began, "everything changed. I knew the magician's trade, but people seemed to think I knew more, that I was holding back some special trick they wanted. I could see it in their faces when I made things appear and disappear. Oh they applauded, of course. And paid well. I had endless tricks, but they were never enough. They wanted something else. But what? I had no answer. No such wisdom. Years went by like this till the name 'Zoromagus' was spoken in places long before I ever got there. But by now, whenever they were watching me with awe, I was looking back at them with shame, and all the time asking myself — what is it? What is it?"

He turned to me. "Have you ever noticed how long a simple, obvious truth can dangle right in front of your face before you finally bump your head against it?"

I can't explain why I felt so sure of the explanation that popped into my head just then, my last answer to a direct question having gone so wide of the mark. It may have been the memory of that power I felt on the veranda when the idea of camping out occurred to me, or else those reflective minutes over a darkened billiard table. In any case, the confidence I heard in my own voice surprised me.

"Yes," I said. "Your magic was a substitute. They saw you turn things into something else. They wanted you to turn them into something else."

"You grow wise, my young friend," he said, and I felt him slip his arm through mine.

"It came to me once from the humblest of teachers," he went on. "Maybe the wisest too. I was staying at a grand hotel in Constantinople. Ee-stahn-bool if you must. Twice the footmen and foolery of this place. To get to the villa where I was supposed to perform you had to pass through an open marketplace. There was a fruit stand. So I stopped. Without thinking, I made a coin pop into my hand. Like this."

He flicked his fingers and a small, lead-colored coin appeared. He pressed it into my palm, and I slid it into my pocket. (I have carried it to this day. Looking at it before me now, I know the Arabic letters cupped in the crescent by heart, though I still have no idea of their meaning.)

"Anyway," he continued, "someone shouted 'Zoromagus', and a crowd gathered. They were friendly enough, smiling and touching me. Most were pretty dirty, and let me say – rank. But I could see that I was never going to get through that mass of bodies unless I gave them some sort of show. My equipment was in a trunk on its way to the villa, but I had a few things about me. One trick led to another. I wound up giving the performance of my life. Never made it to the villa."

My companion and I were in step together by now, arm in arm.

"But you still haven't explained yet," I protested.

"I'm getting there," he said. "By this time there were children up front, little boys with wooden swords and girls too young to cover their faces, all squeezing between the adults to see. There was one little girl. Her mother or someone was pushing her up front. I could see by her face that she wasn't normal. Squinty eyes, face all puffy, mouth half open. The girl, I mean. Couldn't see the woman's face. Covered up, you know. Ever been to a Muslim country?" he asked.

"No," I said, "but go on."

"I put my handkerchief in my pocket then pulled it out of my hat. Had one in those days. Anyway, when I did that, I saw her hop. Boop! Like that. And she clapped her hands. It was like a call. Ever felt a call, Tom?"

"No Sir, I haven't," I said.

"Well, from that moment on I was performing just for her like we were the only two souls in the whole marketplace," he said. "I got down on the stones in front of her and started going faster and faster, one trick on top of another till there was so much noise around me I though I'd go deaf. But her eyes, Tom, they got bigger and bigger till they were the most beautiful eyes I had ever seen. And mine were getting just as big. I kept thinking 'my eyes are open too. They're open wide now', and my hands and fingers were just flying.

And then an idea flew into my head. I stopped, and it got quiet all around. I took this finger here and slid it into her open mouth, back on her tongue. I was going to pull out a coin. Actually, that very one I just gave you. But somehow it wasn't in my palm where it had to be for the trick to work. When I pulled my finger out, she was laughing. And then – she shouted something out loud. Can't say what. Didn't know the language. But all of a sudden there was screaming and excitement all around and a whole shower of coins bouncing off me onto the stones."

"Why," I asked. "What was it?"

"Well," he said, "there was a merchant there who spoke a sort of Greek-Italian mix. He explained to me that up to that moment she had never once spoken a word from the day she was born." He took a deep breath, then added, "After that I had to spend some time out in the hills by myself."

"Yes," I said. "Forty days in the wilderness. You went to seek God."

"Nothing of the sort," he said. "The prefect who owned the villa was furious because I never showed up. Ruined his party. I had to get out of town. Lost my trunk and everything. But it did give me a few days to think. Hunger clears the mind, you know."

I thought of my little food stash up behind the hotel. "When is the last time you ate," I asked.

"None of your business," he snapped. "Let me go on. There's more."

We were still arm in arm, but walking faster now, pulled along by the momentum of his story.

"There was a good-sized lake," he was saying, "like this place but no mountains. Had orchards around it. I borrowed a few olives and dates and drank the water. My last night out there I stayed out by the shore till dawn."

I must confess here that, as I listened to him, I was waiting for a description of some vision or voice, some brilliant but unnatural light from above. At that time in my young life I still imagined that such things were possible, that under the right circumstances I, myself, could be so selected, and that such a likelihood, however remote, was not likely to be just a byproduct of innocence and arrogance. I held my breath for a dozen steps up the pathway, imagining thunder or an angel choir.

"Could have been the olives," he said, "but I

began to think from down here instead of up here." He hugged the shoes up against his middle. "Kept thinking of myself down on my knees in front of that little girl, making her eyes grow like that and putting my finger on her tongue. And just like that, I knew for sure that I loved her, and I loved her mother or whoever she was for bringing her to me, and I loved the people who must have told her I was there, and the ones who watched me get down to do what I did and shouted and threw the coins, and the ones who told the prefect where I had been, and the prefect, himself, who had me run out of town and his minions all. And I could see clear as sunlight that I had never been so happy ever before as when I was down on my knees on the stones there. And all at once, from that very moment, I knew what I was going to do and who I was going to be all the rest of my life."

It was an impressive speech, and it took me a moment to answer. "What did you do then?" I asked.

"I threw up in the lake and passed out," he said. "Woke up with the sun in my eyes and saw an angel fanning me with his wings."

"An angel!" I exclaimed.

He grinned. "Turned out it was just the farmer swatting me with a palm branch."

"Easy enough to make a mistake like that," I said, looking straight ahead.

"After that I didn't do as many villas and fancy theatres," he continued. "I worked more on the streets. That's how I came across Mister so-called Zoromagus back there. I'd been working the streets for a number of years by then and was doing prisons and asylums too. When he came along, I started teaching him, and pretty soon we were working together. He'd been in trouble most of his life for being a little light-fingered, if you get my meaning. Magic put that to good use. And let me say, he was good. Very good." He dropped his voice and added, "Up to a point, that is."

"What was his name then," I asked, "or his real name now, or whichever?"

"William," he said. "William C. Wooley. I called him 'Willie'."

"Willie Wooley, Wooly Willie," I said out loud and laughed. "What's the 'C' stand for?"

"Nothing," he replied. "He stuck it in because he thought it sounded more like he had some family, which he didn't, sad to say, except me of course."

I stopped laughing and tried to imagine the swaggering, bejeweled figure I had seen on stage as a callow street urchin. The transformation must have been a pretty good trick on its own.

"But you were a father to him," I offered.

"Yes," he said simply.

"Fathers and sons don't always get along," I

said. "You must have had a falling out."

He made no answer.

By this time we had climbed to the far end of the lake and come to the edge of a circular, flagstone plaza. The tower stood at the center. This was a round, medieval revival affair of stone, about thirty feet in diameter at the base and tapering upward as a truncated cone to a height of six or more stories. Narrow, vertical slits of windows at staggered intervals indicated a spiral staircase inside. There appeared to be an open parapet or platform at the top, surrounded by a crenellated stone wall. Down at the base, the plaza extended a good thirty-five feet on all sides, suggesting a moat. This was bordered by a low, circular wall, probably meant as a bench for weary climbers. It had an opening at the end of the footpath where we stood and another for an exit on the opposite side. There was a carved wooden sign, legible in the moonlight.

"The Tower of a Hundred Steps," I read out loud.

We stood there a moment, studying this huge anachronism. It struck me as a gigantic charcoal drawing come to life, with one side in moonlight and the other shaded into darkness. I had labored over such a drawing as a small boy, smudging my fingers and face with soot, and here I had come upon it again.

Either he read my thoughts or was finally speaking to the question I had asked a few moments before, but my friend startled me by saying, "Good and evil lie very closely together, much as light and shadow." Then he added, "When the world turns, one can become the other." And before I could think of a reply, he had darted ahead of me.

"A hundred, eh?" he called out. "Let's count 'em."

There was no interior chamber inside the open door, only the stairway winding up to the right between stone walls no more than a yard apart. He went up in front of me, surprisingly quick for his age and the darkness. I struggled to stay close, following the sound of his padding feet and running my hands along the walls for guidance. There was a faint trickle of water somewhere, and breeze hummed softly as we passed each sliver of a window. As we passed the ones on the moonlit side he would appear then disappear quickly, first a glimmer of his hair and old suit and then just his bare heels bouncing up ahead of me.

We climbed without talking, each keeping his separate count until we emerged onto the heavy planks of the open platform with only the night sky above us.

"An even hundred," he shouted over the breeze.

"I counted ninety-nine," I panted.

"Must have missed something along the way," he replied. He didn't seem the least bit winded.

"Yes," I said. "It's the part about how you and your young disciple went your separate ways."

He laughed. "Yes," he said, "you did miss that." He placed his shoes carefully on the wooden floor and slid down to sit beside them, using the stone wall as a windbreak and backrest. I sat beside him.

"Thomas, I believe we have entered a magic circle," he said. "Only truth may be spoken here. And we may see visions."

Indeed, it was a circle, about twenty feet across. The crenellated stone wall of blocks separated by gaps surrounded us like a miniature Stonehenge. The pagan implication did not escape me. The moon had descended more now so that I could see it framed in one of the wall gaps across from us as my friend began his explanation.

"You see," he said, "there is the illusion of magic, and then there is magic, real magic."

I tensed. This is what Maurel had said. But the old fellow went on.

"I call it magic because there's no rational explanation for it. It just is. Like us. Some call it magic because they're afraid of it. It can control you, upsets lots of things, gets in the way of plans and personal ambition. It can get you killed."

"I'm not sure I know what you're talking about," I said.

"I'm talking about the God-given power to care about others like they were your own precious hide," he said. "That sound so new to you?"

"No," I said. "I just never thought of it as magic before."

"What else could it be?" he asked. "It defies logic. Flies in the face of nature. Survival of the fittest and all that. Therein lies our difference."

It took me a second to realize he meant with William C. Wooley rather than me.

"I had learned how to call people out by performing for them," he said, "especially the uncared for, the uncared about. The magic in me went out through my hands into their eyes, their ears, their mouths. I made them see it and believe it, believe that there's nothing, nothing on this little round ball of earth that can't become something different from what it appears to be or what it's been taught to be. It can all – all be changed."

Of course, I thought. It was so simple now. And without realizing that I had gotten up, I found myself walking around the circle in the dark, nodding to no one in particular. The moon was almost entirely down at this point and, as I looked out, I saw that a couple of lanterns had been lit down by the hotel.

Finally I asked, "Does Zoromagus, I mean

Willie, disagree?"

"He didn't then," he said, "at least not openly. We traveled many years as a pair, and we were good together, very good. Then over the years, I began to think I was getting old, much older than my father when he died. So we came to an agreement, he and I. Care to guess?"

"You would retire and he would become Zoromagus," I said.

"Yes," he said. "That was it exactly."

"What went wrong?"

He was slow to answer. In the distance a pair of lanterns looked like cat's eyes.

"I made two mistakes," he said. "The first was that I hadn't prepared him as well as I thought. Magic is power, but power comes with temptation. When it becomes power over others instead of love of others, then there's no more real magic. It's just the illusion of magic. And this becomes an even bigger temptation, not just because it's easier to do, but because having power over others leads to the damnedest illusion of all."

"Which is?"

"The illusion that you're better than others. When that happens, you can do terrible things," he said, then repeated himself softly. "Terrible things."

The lanterns had multiplied by now and were moving alongside the hotel where we had been over an hour ago. Night watchmen, I thought. We might meet them on our way back and have to explain our presence here.

"Parents can't always tell how their children will turn out," I said. "Mine sent me to college to prepare for the ministry. Willie isn't even your real child." I regretted this last statement as soon as I said it and tried to shift the conversation.

"You said there were two things, two mistakes," I said. When my companion didn't answer right away, I sat beside him again and waited.

"I gave him the name," he said finally. "That was easy to let go. But I found that I couldn't let him go. 'Let me go with you,' I said. 'I'll stand back and let you work. I won't interfere. You're Zoromagus now.' But he wouldn't hear of it. He had younger friends, associates. It was all different now. I was in the way. So we parted. Over the years I heard about him from others, where he was, what his work was like, what he was becoming."

"Is that why you've come here?" I asked. "To do something about it? Maybe get your name back?"

"No," he said. "It's far too late for that. Besides, it means something else now. I wouldn't want it."

"Then why come?" I asked. "Why follow him all the way up here to be treated like this?" He had been talking very softly. I leaned toward him to hear better.

"Because," he said, "because I still love him."

We fell silent again for a while. If he meant more than simply as a father loves a son I cannot say, for in those days I knew very little of the many facets of love, though either way it is of no consequence to me now. And so I chose to sit by him in the darkness with our shoulders touching, imagining that my youth might provide him some small comfort in the face of his old loss.

We sat like that for what seemed a good while. Eventually, I broke our silence with a question.

"What will you do now?" I said. "Where will you go?"

"I'll just go on," he said, "somewhere, for whatever time is left."

I felt a pang at that.

"What can I do?" I asked. Then realizing that it was a much bigger question than I had realized, I asked more pointedly, "I mean — what do I do? What do I do from here on?"

It seemed as though the breeze around us had stopped, so that the night was holding its breath with me.

"Put them on your shoulders," he said. "Put them on your shoulders, and you will fly."

I wasn't sure what he meant, but if his instruction was what I took it to be, I thought it a hopeless task. I had none of his particular skill. For that matter, it seemed to me that I had no notable skill of any kind whatsoever. I got up and crossed the circle again, feeling ahead of me for the wall and trying to imagine myself flying out over the lake to where the moon had disappeared.

But now there were multiple flickers of lantern light among the trees where the footpath approached the tower plaza. Not workman, I thought. Our privacy was going to be ruined by a party of revelers.

"There's someone coming," I said. "I think there's a pack of them."

"Yes," he said. But he showed no sign of getting up to look.

The party burst out of the woods into the open plaza, about ten or a dozen men with several lanterns. From my height, I could see only the tops of their hats, but two of them carried what appeared to be one of the long pieces of lumber from where we had been sitting out on the dock. They sat it down noisily at the foot of the tower. There was some milling around.

"We should leave," I said.

"No," he replied. "You may though."

I leaned forward through one of the stone gaps to see better. Two or three had taken off their hats, possibly to wipe their faces after their rapid climb. One of them pulled something dark over his head and face, then another did the same, then a third. Now I saw a flash of copper hair in the lantern light.

"Damn it all," I said aloud and spun around. "You stay here. I'm going down."

That moment when I spoke to him in the darkness stands out especially in my present memory. I never saw him again.

The stairway was totally black this time. I slipped and caught myself against the walls several times on my downward race. I wanted to stop them at the door. When I practically toppled out onto the plaza, I was in the midst of a pack of faceless men. They wore the black hoods with the gold symbols.

"Maurel!" I shouted. "Maurel! For God's sake, which one are you?"

One of them holding a lantern hooked my arm and led me aside. When he pulled off his hood, I saw it was Maurel.

"Otis, my friend," he said, "I tried to warn you more than once. Now you'll have a chance to see some justice done."

I thought he smelled of alcohol. "What are you saying?" I demanded. He was smiling in his characteristic pose, head back and teeth displayed, this time holding the lantern for his own stage effect. I wanted to hit him in the mouth.

"We have an uninvited trespasser to deal with," he said. "Your Mr. Ferency is not a guest here. He never registered at the hotel. Wouldn't be allowed to anyway. But he's been on private hotel property the whole time. We're going to send him on his way."

Behind me, most of the others had entered the tower and were running up the stairs. By the lantern in Maurel's hand I could see the long plank they had dropped by the door. Next to it were a couple of the hotel pillows and a bucket. I recognized it as one of the wallpaper paste buckets I had seen outside my room.

What these bullies had in mind was immediately clear!

"No you won't," I yelled and ran into the tower.

They had a head start on me, but I shoved my way roughly past several on the narrow stairs and ran ahead of their shouts and curses. This time it seemed like two hundred steps. When I burst onto the open platform, two of them were leaning over the wall, holding out lanterns.

My friend was nowhere to be seen.

"Oh my God!" I screamed. "What have you done to him?"

They had pulled off their hoods to see better. Others were still arriving.

"I got here first," one said. "I saw him go over."

"I saw it too," another said. "The old goat

jumped from right here. I saw his coat tail go over just as I got to the top step."

I darted over and leaned out at the spot. There was only darkness. When I whirled around I was face to face with Zoromagus. He was holding the shoes.

"Wooley, you scum!" I snarled. Even by lamplight, I could see that he was ashen. His mouth was moving but no words came out.

I made a dive for the doorway just as Maurel arrived with his lantern. I grabbed it and shoved him out of the way. He went sprawling. I half ran, half tumbled my way down the stairwell, shielding the lantern with my elbows. Once I lost my footing entirely, spun completely around and slammed into the stone, bouncing off like a billiard ball. I shot out the door and circled the tower on a dead run holding the lantern out in front of me.

Then I circled again in a wider radius and finally ran around on top of the low bench surrounding the plaza, peering out at all the nearby ground.

My friend was nowhere to be seen.

I came back toward the tower and stared up dizzily. It narrowed toward to top so that one would have to leap forward several feet just to clear the base of the wall. The plaza was another thirty-five feet wide. No man leaps that distance I knew.

It was as though he had never landed! As if he had flown!

Suddenly there was a fluttering sound above me. Something was banging down the side of the tower. I jumped back in panic just as my derby landed at my feet.

It occurred to me at this point that I might be in some danger myself. These fellows had missed their quarry by a seeming miracle, but I could be seen as an accomplice. There was almost a dozen of them, and I had already handed out a few bruises. My press role would be little protection. I snatched up my hat, snuffed the lantern, tossed it away and stumbled out the opposite side of the plaza onto the pathway that continued down and around the other side of the lake.

There was no way to run in the pitch black, but I managed a brisk walk, holding my arms out in front of me like a sleepwalker, gauging the sound of my shoes on the path, and following the gaps between the overhead branches where the stars became visible. About a hundred yards along I stopped to listen. There was only darkness and soft wind. What had happened must have taken the heart out of them for any more bullying.

When I had crept along for about half an hour I passed what must have been an opening in the trees because lanterns were visible across the lake. The would-be assailants were retracing their steps back to the hotel. They seemed to halt periodically, so that I was able to keep up a parallel course with them, even without benefit of a light. I imagined that they might have been arguing among themselves. There would be no crime to conceal without a body, of course. Still, I took grim satisfaction at the thought of William C. Wooley struggling to rationalize all this before his pack of disciples.

The path descended, and I came to another open space directly opposite the hotel. I remembered that there was a wooden catwalk here, on top of boulders that jutted out from the lakeshore. Flashes of lantern light were visible against the boathouse across the water. I found the railing to the catwalk and crept out along the planks to the end. Then I lay down on my stomach to watch.

The lanterns had dwindled to a single light by now, and that one was moving out in my direction on the central boat dock across the lake. I couldn't tell who carried it. The figure raised an arm and seemed to hurl something. There was a faint splash, then another. It had to be the shoes, I thought. But whether they were thrown to conceal evidence or as an act of exorcism I would never know. In a moment, figure and light were both gone.

And then I was alone in the darkness with my even darker rage.

10

As I write today, it is all too clear to me that any normal person reading this account would take me for a madman or a liar. To be sure, some of the events I have described might seem just as well to have been drawn from The Arabian Nights or the Brothers Grimm. I can only assure anyone who cares to dwell on these pages that I would not have written a word of my adventure were it not accurate to the best of my memory and true in the sense that light, love, and life itself are true. Moreover, what I must now add to my witness includes an experience that most will find more fantastic yet, though I could not do justice to this overall account were I to omit it.

Alone in the dark, I had lost all sense of time. I guessed that night was largely past, but I had no watch with me, nor could I have seen the dial anyway. The heat of the previous day was long gone, and I had been sitting cross-legged at the end of the catwalk, hunched against the chill with my jacket collar up for what seemed like hours. It would have been warmer back in the shelter of the trees, but staying here, where I had seen what I thought was the conclusion of the night's events, gave me a sense that it was still before my eyes, still accessible to my senses if not my reason. And so I sat like an arctic Buddha in chilly meditation.

If I had seen something miraculous, I was not the first to have had that experience. History, folklore, and the Bible are full of such. Nor was I repelled by the irrational aspect. I had been drawn to magic for some time now, and it was dawning on me that I had harbored such a penchant for most of my young life. My attraction to the inexplicable had led me to organized religion, just as my impatience with pomp and pretense had turned me away from it.

What bothered me now on top of the violence I had just experienced was a sense of fraudulence, a suspicion that I had tricked and cheated my way into a spot that was not rightfully mine. While Wooley and his cadre were abashed and angered to be shown up as mere illusionists, I felt small and humiliated, simply no match for the scope of what I had seen and heard. The arrival of that pack at the tower could well have saved me from trespassing further into secrets where I had no business. In that sense, I was in their debt.

And what of William C. Wooley, the stammering urchin turned grandiose showman, and Maurel, his dandy disciple, and the others, I thought? What nefarious bond drew them together? Any one theory seemed as good as another to me now. And why such hatred for one's protector, one's own past? Wasn't the masked, misnamed and derbied lot of us all stumbling together down one dark path or another as I had just done?

I thought of my friend sitting by that other, faraway lake near an olive orchard and feeling his love for the little girl who spoke her first words and all the people around her, including the angry prefect who had chased him into temporary exile. And as I pondered thus in cross-legged contemplation, I felt my rage slipping away with the night.

Part of it was the dawn. I could make out the gray boulder just below me and minutes later the dark water just in front of it and finally a dense fog that sat like a cloud on the lake surface. When I lay back to watch the sky lighten, there was something hard against my hip, and I pulled the unopened pack of hotel cards out of my pocket. For all my running and near tumbling of the hours before, it had remained where my friend had somehow placed it.

I weighed the small, sealed box in my palm, wishing it were a sandwich or at least a biscuit and smiled at my old, sanctimonious view of these inert toys. Without thinking, I broke open the box and turned the pack over in my hand. For a fraction of a second in that dim light I thought I was looking down into a pocket mirror.

It was not a mirror but a small, tinted photograph of me, staring back at myself!

I gasped. How had he done this? I slid it off to see if the real cards were underneath and saw my mother, just as I had last seen her on our front porch. The next card was my father, holding the reins as he sat on our buggy. Under that were my two brothers in the door of our carriage house with the hayloft above. Then came neighbors and school chums in places just as I remembered.

My hands were shaking, but I couldn't stop going through the deck. Here were my professors and young men my age from college, and now it was Wilson and faces I knew in Baltimore, then suddenly Maurel with his copper hair and Wooley as Zoromagus with his hand under his chin to show his ring.

I went faster and saw people I didn't know, women with their faces covered and a little girl with huge eyes and men in fur parkas and others nearly naked holding long spear shafts with knifelike points, then others in silk robes.

The cards were endless, multiplying as fast as I could go through them. Now I was seeing people with cracked and scarred faces, families of nothing but skin and bone, children with huge swollen heads or distended stomachs, and people of all ages and sizes wrapped in rags with missing noses or fingers and hideous, discolored scabs covering their bodies.

The card at the very bottom was faint, and my hands were shaking so much that I had to put them down in my lap and lean forward to see who it was.

At first, I thought it was my newfound but now lost friend. And then it looked more like me, only older, much older, much as I appear today when looking into my shaving mirror. Then it seemed to be fading into an ordinary face card. I might have called out to my friend at that point. In my excitement, I can't remember.

But now I heard his voice coming out of the fog, or rather it was more like the fog itself had become his voice so that I could feel it vibrating softly against my whole body.

"Put them on your back," he said. "Put them on your back and you will fly."

It brought me to my feet. The cards tumbled out of my lap and into the lake. I peered down and saw them churning up the water as a silver flurry of trout in a feeding frenzy. But when they dove under, they did not disappear from my view, for Looking Glass Lake, once a dark, impenetrable surface, was suddenly light and transparent as open air beneath me.

This lasted only an instant, but in that tiny chink

of time I saw clearly hundreds of feet downward to the ancient bottom of that underwater chasm, through layer below layer of time till I thought I was staring into the very birth of the world. And then it was over. The water was dark glass once more.

Now I was standing just past the end of the catwalk with my feet planted on the rock. I felt as though I had risen to speak out to all the space around me but was waiting for words to say.

Then suddenly, a bird somewhere behind me sang out one long, solitary note.

Another answered.

It was a call.

At that moment the granite beneath me seemed part of my own body so that I bore the whole lake in my arms. I could stretch above the mountain peaks to hold the distant oceans in full view. The earth might have reversed itself upon its axis had I chosen to push off against this boulder.

It did turn for me, in fact, for I spun myself around like a discus thrower and hurled my precious derby out into the fog to join the shoes. If it ever landed, I never heard it.

And starting from that moment, I knew what I was going to do, one way or another, for the rest of my days!

My railroad ticket was still in my wallet. My bag of books and article notes behind the hotel could rot. I was off in a race to catch up with the rest of my life.

Less than a quarter mile more around the lake and I was back on the main road to the Corinth train depot at a brisk trot. It was only about two miles, but I could have run ten.

Writing at this moment, I see it and live it as I did then. The day grows brighter at each twist of the path until I'm bounding along the descent, scattering birds and squirrels as I leap from patch to patch of sunlight. The road levels out just as I hear a train whistle through the trees. I leave the road, crash through the underbrush toward the sound then jump a small embankment.

The train stands fifty yards ahead of me on the southbound track. It's just a local, picking up milk cans and dropping off mail, but there's a passenger coach on the end. The conductor signals to the engineer and swings himself onto the steps of the rear platform. My yell is drowned out by another whistle blast, but when the man turns, I see him smile. He waves me on.

The train is moving now, but the momentum is mine. And here I close the gap in a matter of seconds. I leap aboard.

Sixty years gone but my spirit soars again with the swelling rumble under my feet as I cling to the handrail. Now I am panting and trying to sing I know not what at the top of my bursting lungs. And here I wave an arm to all the world. And finally, I throw my head back as I did then, for once more I am deliberately looking up and into the blinding light of the glorious morning sun.

Acknowledgements

For their help and encouragement, I would like to thank Dan Skoubye, David Abbott, James Benedict, Claudia Orpin, Millicent Fairhurst, Patrick Glass, Philip Spitzer, and my wife, Catherine.

About the Author

W. H. (Hank) Johnson was raised in New York City and educated at Duke and the University of North Carolina. His previous publications include poetry and plays, a number of which have been staged off-off-Broadway, or at regional, civic, or university theatres. He has taught at Skidmore College, Western Michigan University and Towson University and also has been a financial planner, a retail owner-operator, a theatre publicist, a state arts council director, a Chamber of Commerce executive and a Realtor. He lives with his wife in Maryland, where they are restoring an old house.

OTHER

ONE FLIGHT  FICTION™

BOOKS AVAILABLE:

Titles	Read Time
Home To Wyoming	0-1 hour read
Perceptions	0-1 hour read
Summersville	1-2 hour read
Dreamers	2-3 hour read

To give us your feedback and learn more about One Flight Fiction, visit us on the web.

www.OneFlightFiction.com

ONE FLIGHT  FICTION™

Banda Press International, Inc. is proud to present
ONE FLIGHT FICTION™

Perhaps you've thumbed through a magazine trying to find something to read. Or maybe you've found yourself flying from Phoenix to Dallas, with more paperwork than you can imagine awaiting your arrival. Starting a novel (that you'll never finish) just doesn't seem to cut it. Whether on a two hour flight or on a tight schedule at home; *One Flight Fiction*™ will afford you the luxury of curling up with a good book and finishing it, in less than three hours!

We look forward to filling the gap between magazines and novels; and providing you with
ONE FLIGHT FICTION™

Visit us
at
www.OneFlightFiction.com